PRESENTED BY

SUE AND RANDY PARKER
IN HONOR OF
OUR DAUGHTER
LEAH PARKER
2002

Taylor Bremer
2002

WESTMINSTER SCHOOLS   SMYTHE GAMBRELL LIBRARY

Cats of Myth

American Shorthair
of the Americas

British Shorthair
of Europe

Egyptian
Mau of Africa

Siamese
of Asia

Cats OF Myth

TALES FROM AROUND THE WORLD

Gerald & Loretta Hausman

Illustrated by Leslie Baker

SIMON & SCHUSTER BOOKS FOR YOUNG READERS

New York   London   Toronto   Sidney   Singapore

For Rebecca Davis
—G. H. and L. H.

For Clarence, Rome, Princess, Apollo, Pretty Boy, Peach Pit,
Harriet, Seymour, Grey One, Red One, Alice, Amanda,
Oliver, and, lastly, the beautiful Nellie
—L. B.

ARTIST'S NOTE

The illustrations in this book were painted on 140-pound cold press Lanaquarelle paper. The paper is stretched after the completion of a simple pencil sketch, then painted in transparent watercolor using wet techniques and layered washes. Occasionally, gouache is used. I work with a fairly limited palette, favoring Winsor Newton, Sennelier, and Holbein paints.

SIMON & SCHUSTER BOOKS FOR YOUNG READERS
An imprint of Simon & Schuster Children's Publishing Division
1230 Avenue of the Americas, New York, New York 10020

Book design by Anahid Hamparian
The text for this book is set in 14-point Venetian.
Printed in Hong Kong

2 4 6 8 10 9 7 5 3 1

Library of Congress Cataloging-in-Publication Data
Hausman, Gerald.
Cats of myth : tales from around the world / by Gerald and Loretta Hausman ;
illustrated by Leslie Baker.
p. cm.
Includes bibliographical references.
Summary: A collection of stories from Egypt, India, Japan, Scandinavia, Ireland and other places
that portray cats as goddesses, guardians, tricksters, warriors, magicians, and more.
ISBN 0-689-82320-7
1. Cats—Folklore. 2. Tales. [1. Cats—Folklore. 2. Folklore.] I. Hausman, Loretta.
II. Baker, Leslie A., ill. III. Title.
PZ8.1.H29 Cat 2000
398.24'529752—dc21
99-48472

Contents

Introduction: A Cat's-Eye Tapestry of Mythology

If a cat were to write a history of humans, we're certain it would be fairer to us than we, in our literature, have been to them. *Cats of Myth* seeks to set this score aright by recounting some of our oldest and most mystical stories that venerate cat magic. Herein, we've presented the elusive feline as goddess, guardian, guide, trickster, warrior, rescuer, magician, and overall mistress of humanity.

Beginning in ancient Egypt, we find the friendly feline worshiped in the valley of the Nile. Adored for her insightful eye, the cat was imitated by women, who used kohl as catlike eyeliner. Men, too, likened themselves to cats when they shaved their eyebrows as a sign of mourning whenever a cat died. Egyptian soldiers in foreign lands were required to catch all the cats they saw and bring them home. Our story "Bast, the Cat Goddess" is an actual historical tale about a bloody war that was ended all because of the Egyptian Mau.

Other stories featuring the mystic powers of the farseeing feline as she went from the Middle East to Europe are "Spiegel and the Cat's Grease" and "The Tale of the Whittle Cat." Each of these tells about the European Shorthair and her special kind of cat magic. Women of the Rhineland met in sacred groves under the high moon and worshiped Freya, the Nordic goddess of love and fertility, just like the people of the Nile. Sometimes, however, as in our two tales, cat power can get out hand—or paw, as the case might be.

In Asia, the feline was also sacred and a personal guardian of royalty.

She stored the souls of departing rulers in her breast and carried them to the next world. Our story "The Temple Cat of Lao-Tsun" comes from the mountains of Burma and features the Birman breed. This seventeenth-century tale presents the cat as heavenly caretaker as well as earthly adviser.

Other guardian cat tales in *Cats of Myth* travel across the centuries to the Bahamian Islands and show us an unusual portrait of Calico Jack, the pirate, and the American Shorthair that saved his life by introducing him to a dolphin and a mer-girl.

What all of these enchanted myths seem to be saying is that cats, whether practical, comical, mystical, or historical, are as close to us today as when the first Egyptian bowed to the tall, cat-shaped Bast on the banks of the Nile. We are still worshipers, and these nine tales are dedicated to the nine lives of our most special feline friend.

The Creation Cat

The Tiger and the Tabby: An East Indian Folktale

A long time ago there was a tiger and her best friend, a tabby cat. This was the time of beginnings, when people lived separate from animals but all creatures of the forest lived together. Now, as for the tiger and the tabby, they were never apart. And when they walked side by side, their stripes converged, and they looked like black water on fire-colored sand. Apart from each other, one was just a miniature version of the other.

They lived, these two, in perfect harmony. The tiger hunted large animals and brought them to their den. The tabby caught mice and other rodents, and these, though small, he shared with his friend. The tabby also usually stayed at home and kept their cave clean by sweeping it with his tail.

One day the tiger came home, shivering. Her stripes slithered across her back like so many writhing snakes.

"Sister," said the tabby. "You have a sickness inside you. Lie down in the back of the cave and I will bring you something to drink."

The tiger said, "I am very cold."

"It is the fever in your bones," explained the tabby, but his friend did not care what it was, so long as she might be rid of it. "Help me, brother," she said, and she lay down with a tiger's terrible resignation.

At once, the tabby bounded out of the cave. "I must find the thing called fire. It is the only remedy for my sister's illness."

He came to a village at the edge of a thorn tree plain. There, in the smoke-smudged dusk, he spied a mud house, within which lived a family of human beings. Carefully he threaded his way through the thorny yard. The family, fearful of wild animals, had scattered bullhorn stickers all round the house. It was through these that the cat wove his sinewy way.

"For my sister," he said under his breath, "I would do anything because I know she would do anything for me."

Through an open window the tabby saw the thing called fire. It did a pretty dance, all by itself, in a little cave set into the wall.

It is laughable, thought the tabby, *how much the fire likes itself. And how, I wonder, do I steal a thing that dances to its own tune—and with no visible partner? Truly it is some magic that makes it do so.*

For a long while the cat stayed. He watched, considering what to do next. Finally, on cat-quiet feet, he crept between the slumbering human forms that lay on fiber mats about the room. He made no sound. Soon he was at the cave of light, wherein the fire danced.

A container of milk mixed with crushed cardamom, honey, and black tea was sitting in the hot ashes. Beside it was a red clay dish in which there was a roasted fish. The aroma that came from these treats was so delectable that the tabby put his white face close. Pleased, he drank in their fragrance.

Sniffing, he stared raptly at the fire. The silly flames danced on, unaware that anyone was there. So the tabby took a nibble of the fish. It was very agreeable. He dipped his sandpaper tongue into the milk drink, and it, too, was fine to the taste.

"This is sweeter than dew from the temple tree," said the tabby, licking the droplets from his chin.

One taste led to another.

Soon the warm fish and the sweet drink made the tabby sleepy. He grew heavy-lidded. *I have come a long way,* he reasoned, *and I am tired. Better I should rest now than be caught by a wolf, or a snake, on the prowl.*

So, forgetting about his sister, the tabby dropped off to sleep in front of the warm, drowsy fire.

Back in the cave, the tiger rose. She roared in pain. She was burning and freezing at the same time. She slashed her tail, hither and yon.

Far off, her fire-comforted friend, the dozing tabby, drifted from one pleasant dream to another. Suddenly he dreamed that his sister was calling him. He blinked sleepily. Then, stretching before the fire's warmth, he slept some more.

So it was that this master of the wilderness had already become a servant of comfort.

The tiger, meanwhile, resigned herself to the dead banyan leaves in the dank darkness. Lying down, she accepted her misery. But she let go one last violent roar, which made even the pampas grass quiver.

The tiger's anguish stirred the sleeping tabby.

Startled, the tabby awoke.

And suddenly he remembered what he had come to do.

The fire was banked low in the hearth. Quickly the tabby grabbed a red-tipped firestick with his teeth. Then he rushed like the dawn wind back to his ailing sister. Through the raw, gray morning he tore at full tilt, arriving at the tiger's side before the first rays of the sun touched the cave mouth.

Instantly the tiger raised her boldly patterned face. The old, arrogant eyes flashed angrily. "I thought you'd never come," said she. And she sadly rested her white chin upon her orange-and-black paws.

"I beg your forgiveness, sister. But, I must tell you, the fire-thing was so warm, the milk so sweet, the fish so good . . . oh, I ate until I was full, and then, I must say, I dropped off to sleep."

"Did you bring me any of these wonderful things to eat?" the tiger demanded.

"Sorry, I did not. There was no time. I took this firestick, however, and I will now show you how it can dance."

Hastily the tabby gathered dead leaves and sticks from the tiger's bed. Then he breathed upon the glow-stick. The smoldering end alighted the tinder. A fresh little fire was born and it bathed the cave in lemon-bright light.

"This is well and good," said the famished tiger bitterly. "But I need some food to eat, and I am too weak to catch anything."

"I promise to bring you some fine food—next time."

The fire burnished the cave. It danced and did tricks. The tabby went out into the bush and caught tree frogs for the tiger, who ate them down, small though they were.

After a time, the tiger recovered. But the fire went out, and the tabby could not get it going again.

Secretly he yearned for the mud house, and the delicious food that was stored there. The cave was cold. Whatever they ate had to be caught, and this was always tiresome. So, one night while catching mice in the meadow, he remembered the roasted fish, the hot, sweet milk. His thoughts returned again to the safety of the mud house and the fire within. And he decided that, undoubtedly, a human house is the right place for a cat.

A few days later, he said to the tiger, "Tonight, I'll catch some sweet, scampering mice."

He spoke softly, subtly. The tiger, raising her great, sad head, knew something was about to happen.

Curiously she watched her brother fade into the night grass. She continued to stare until he was gone. Her sorrowful yellow eyes bore through the night and into tomorrow, and across the days into the future. "I am alone now," she said with resignation. "And I'll never see my brother again."

Thus a sadness she could not see across filled her heart.

As before, the tabby crept into the mud house. The fire was there, dancing. He looked with satisfaction on the leaping light, and then, seeing the masters of the place were all aslumber, ate the food they'd stored in the warm ash. Afterward he lay before the flames, in contentment.

From that point on, he lived a life of ease. Occasionally the two would meet in the tall grass. There was a flicker, a memory of their life together, of the time when their stripes moved with matched precision. Yet between the wild and the tamed there is as much distance as the space between the stars.

Still, in the tabby there remains the wild wisp of the tiger, even today. And in the tiger, some say, there is the friendly twitch of the tabby's tail.

AFTERWORD

The tabby cat may very well be our oldest cat, for it can be traced back to the ancient Kaffir cat of Africa. The Kaffir is a yellowish, striped feline, Felis lybica, *which is yet wild, and lives in Africa today. The Romans brought the Egyptian cat, a mixture of Kaffir and Mau, to England sometime before the fifth century. Our modern tabby is probably a cross between this old mixed breed and the British wildcat.*

The tabby coloration is similar to a pattern of watered silk that came from Turkey many hundreds of years ago. The cat was named after the silk that was spun in Attabiah, a district of old Baghdad where Jewish cloth makers created a fine black-and-white silk that had a watered look to it. When the fabric first appeared in Great Britain, it was called tabbi. Subsequently, people using the silk began to call the similarly patterned cat a "tabby."

Characteristically, the tabby is a hearth cat, a barn cat, a good-luck cat, any kind of cat you care to name, because just about every breed has a variety with a tabby coat. The tabby marking does look a little like a tiger's stripes, hence the relationship in our story.

The Trickster Cat

The Troll King and the Butter Cat:

A Scandinavian Folktale

There was once a legendary cat known as the Butter Cat. You may think you've seen her, perhaps, on your kitchen counter. One lick and the butter's round-shouldered. Well, that's not a true Butter Cat, just a cat that likes to lick butter, as most if not all cats do.

However, we are speaking now of that plump puss of Norway. A farm cat, really, one whose job is to keep mice out of the barn in the summertime. She gets her nickname because in the wintertime her post is on the table by the butter larder.

Guardian of the butter? Yes, but she's more than that. A kitchen cat, then? Yes, that and more. Guardian of hearth and home? Now, that's the thing. She watches over all that happens in the kitchen, including that which human eyes overlook or—to put it plainly—can't quite see.

Well, here is a story that explains why this kind of cat knows the butter from the batter and the hitter from the hatter. In other words, a smarter cat was never born.

Long ago there was a fat old troll king named Rumble Grumble. He got that name because when he was angry, his voice sounded like coal rumbling down a chute, or like an avalanche of snow, or like a tree torn out by the roots in a terrible storm.

Rumble Grumble was bad, bad news. Even the wickedest of the troll people kept out of his cranky way. No wonder, for he was horrible to look at, too. His mossy hair was matted, his teeth were rotten, and his breath was odious. Moreover, Rumble Grumble was hairy and fat, and he had to let out his belt after every meal.

Now, there was another mountain troll named Sweet Butter, who enjoyed the company of Rumble Grumble's wife. This troll was, like his name, nice. He liked to sit in the sun and smoke a small clay pipe, and he minded his own business. But he did have a fondness for hot birch tea, and he liked to drink it with Mrs. Rumble Grumble.

Each day, he stopped by to visit her. Together, they had a cup of that clear, brook-colored tea. Some say that these two fell in love under Rumble Grumble's nose. However, he was too busy squelching people, and never seemed to notice. In the end, though, he caught on, and after roaring and rumbling his rage, he banished Sweet Butter to a dreadful place—the land of humans.

Well, Sweet Butter decided to make the best of things, and he changed himself into a Norwegian Forest Cat with cinnamon fur and dark tabby markings, and a full, bushy tail as long as his body. Cats, he'd heard, were well fed by farmers. So he took himself to a farmhouse that was set at the bottom of a big, sprucy mountain.

The house was made of logs, hand-hewn by the old farmer when he was young. His name was Olaf, and his wife was Sonja, and they loved animals, but none better than cats.

So, Sweet Butter had come to the right place.

Sonja doted on her cat so much that, in time, he hardly ever left the kitchen of the little cabin. There he took up residence on the top shelf of the great porcelain stove, which, all winter long, was warm with the baking of caraway seed bread. On the table in a wooden well was a sandefjord butter server, but though he licked it once or twice, he rarely made a habit of it. For he was regularly served steamed salmon, kjottkaker meat cakes with creamed cabbage, and plenty of sardines on bread. Life couldn't have been better—well, that is, life in the land of humans.

Now, it seemed that Sweet Butter brought his own kind of country bounty to the farm. Never before had the garden yielded such large, towheaded cabbages. Nor had the old cow given such huge amounts of milk and thick, buttery cream.

Indeed, the mice shrank in size—or so it seemed—and the polecats stayed far away. Sweet Butter was a kind of lord of the log house, and the humble dwelling became heaven on earth for Olaf and Sonja. Their neighbors noticed it, too, and came calling. Stig Sovik and his wife, Christiana, called every fortnight to sit by the glowing stove and drink aquavit.

Sweet Butter liked being in their presence because they laughed a lot. Humans, he thought, were at their best when they laughed. Stroking his fire-warmed fur, the Soviks would feed him a double-yoked, hard-boiled egg, which they got from their prize goose.

After a time—a number of years, people say—Sweet Butter quite forgot that he was a troll who had changed himself into a cat. But, though his life was richly rewarding, he still sought the one thing he dearly missed—Rumble Grumble's wife. One day, he vowed, he'd marry her.

Now, all went smoothly for Sweet Butter and his human family until one Christmas morning. Who do you think showed up for Christmas breakfast?

Rumble Grumble.

As everyone knows, you do not refuse a visiting troll anything, for that can mean a lifetime of bad luck. Well, on this particular holiday, Rumble Grumble, who smelled something that he could not quite put his claw on, ate every crumb of food the farmer's wife had on her table.

He gobbled up pounds of pancakes, smeared with cloudberry jam. He glugged down a pail of fresh milk, and he crunched up a huge rasher of bacon. The berries dripped purple on his tobacco-stained beard. Belching, Rumble Grumble looked around. He sniffed the air. His troll's eye missed nothing, you see, and a troll's nose, covered with warts, is a terror to all who hide from it.

Blink, blink; sniff, sniff.

"Hargh," he coughed, "is it a forest puss I smell?"

"Just the sleepy old Butter Cat we've had these many years," said Sonja, eyeing her cat, who was sleeping behind the stove.

"Yah, yah," said the farmer, trying to sound normal. "Just the old cat we use to mop the floor."

Olaf smiled, but Rumble Grumble didn't.

Instead, Rumble Grumble got up from the table. He tipped a cream pitcher

onto the pine planks and let the cream run into the cracks between the boards.

From behind the stove Sweet Butter knew something was up, but he remained quietly in hiding.

Presently, Rumble Grumble let out another awful belch. "What cat refuses spilled cream?" he asked. The spittle trickled from his mouth as he spoke, but he wouldn't wipe it away.

"Only a cat who cannot smell," said Olaf. "He's so old."

"Yah, it is true," said his good wife.

"Can the old cat not hear?" Rumble Grumble queried.

The two shook their heads.

Rumble Grumble made the worst noise of which he was capable. *"Arrgh-ourrough-grufffrrll!"*

He rumbled so loud that the windowpanes cracked. Then, slopping through the rivers of cream he'd spilled on the floor, he found Sweet Butter flicking the cream from his feet.

Rumble Grumble put his foul mouth beside Sweet Butter's left ear. "Is you a good little kitty-goo?" he coughed.

And, leaning even closer, he rumbled so loud, every pine tree on the mountain did a pirouette. Yet Sweet Butter never moved a muscle.

The troll kept rumbling until that beautiful Christmas day was used up. After which, Rumble Grumble trudged back to troll land. But, for some time afterward he thought about how he was going to pay another visit to the farm the following year. He thought about it with relish.

Sweet Butter thought about next Christmas, too. The more he thought about it, the more he liked it. This time, he was going to give Rumble Grumble a surprise. So that year passed, and Christmas again rolled around.

On Christmas Eve, Sweet Butter wandered up the sprucy mountain and came upon a great, yawning den. He went into it and found a sleeping bear buried in aspen leaves.

Sensing the intruder, the bear forced one eye open. "You had better have a good reason to wake me up, cat," the drowsy bear warned.

"Indeed," Sweet Butter said softly, blinking his amber eyes.

Then he came close to the bear's small, round ear and whispered, "How would you like to sleep in a cozy kitchen that smells of nutmeg and cinnamon, and in which a stove-fire burns all the livelong day and night?"

The bear opened his little eyes and grinned foolishly, but also greedily.

A bit after midnight, Sweet Butter returned to the farmhouse. Behind him, clumping through the crisp, crusted snow, was the bear. Once inside the warm building, Sweet Butter told the bear, "Sleep behind the stove, where no one will see you. Tomorrow morning, when I want you to do the thing I told you about, I will tap you with a wooden butter paddle."

The bear muttered good night and, already snoring, slumped behind the stove.

Now, to make sure Olaf and Sonja would have no misgiving about the trick he was soon to play on his ancient enemy, Sweet Butter sent them a raft of bear dreams. He sat by their pillows and, using his troll's magic, he dreamed them into liking all the bears that ever lived. So that, when Sonja awoke Christmas morning, she said to Olaf, "Happy Bear's Day, dear."

Slipping on his long, woolen socks, he answered, "Happy Bear's Day to you, too, dear."

Breakfast was like the year before: pancakes, cloudberry jam, bacon, and milk. And, just like the preceding year, into the kitchen scuffed the scrofulous troll, Rumble Grumble. "Hargh," he croaked, "the table's set for a king—no, for a troll king!"

Olaf and Sonja sipped their tea in silence and paid the rude troll no mind.

After he'd stuffed himself full of pancakes, smeared berries all over his clotted beard, and crumbled bits of bacon on his shirtfront, he strolled over to the stove. On the bread warmer slept Sweet Butter.

"And how is Norsk Skaukatt doing?" Rumble Grumble said in his gravelly voice.

Sweet Butter stretched his paws and yawned. Lazily, he glanced at the greasy troll, who smelled of so many meals, past and present.

Rumble Grumble growled, "What's the matter? Cat got your tongue?"

Sweet Butter jumped up, grabbed the butter paddle, and, going behind the stove, struck something there.

Then came a noise that made the crockery quiver, for the bear woofed way down deep in his throat.

"What?" bellowed Rumble Grumble, who wasn't used to anyone making a noise without his permission. "No one woofs in my presence, least of all a puss!"

And he rumbled so loud that the glazed pitchers and saucers exploded into shards. Milk jugs blew apart, mirrors cracked, plates disintegrated.

Now Sweet Butter struck the bear again. This time, the bear roared and the sound shook the farmhouse off its foundation.

Rumble Grumble roared back so loudly that frozen streams melted and ran the opposite way.

But the bear bellowed so horribly that the sun spun, the day darkened, and the stars glittered and tittered as never before.

That was when Rumble Grumble threw in the towel—he knew he was defeated.

And worse, a Butter Cat had bested him—for he knew that no troll could make such sounds.

Unable to face his disgrace, he forthwith retired as King of the Trolls. Soon after that, he died of boredom.

As for the bear, he spent his winters behind the stove instead of in a drafty old den. That reward, promised him by Sweet Butter, was what clinched the deal to overthrow the troll. And, as everyone knows, trolls fear nothing in this world except noises louder than trolls, and humiliations from feline foes.

Sweet Butter, as you've already surmised, married Rumble Grumble's wife soon after the old ogre passed on. But he persuaded her to change herself into a cat, which she did, so the two of them could live happily ever after in the cabin of Olaf and Sonja.

However, no trolls ever came to that farmhouse again, and to this day, trolls are still afraid of cats. One feline growl will scare them all the way to next Christmas, and to the Christmas after that.

AFTERWORD

The hero of this tale, the Butter Cat of Norway and Sweden (and as far south as the Netherlands), is a mythical cat that is all but unknown today. The myth is, however, an old one that goes far back in time. Laplanders of Sweden know of it and have their own flavorful and whimsical stories about these mystical animals.

As a breed the Butter Cat is any cat that likes butter—in other words, all cats fit the bill. However, the Norwegian Forest Cat is the only cat indigenous to that part of Scandinavia, and so is the perfect complement to our tale.

One such feline we've known, named Tiger, helped his owners capture a number of finches that had escaped from their cage. Tiger caught them on the wing, outdoors, and brought them inside, unharmed. He carried them gently in his mouth. Tiger is a loner with glittery, humorous, circumspect eyes. One can easily imagine him doing battle with a troll because he is also fiercely intelligent and combative to a degree that is rare in other cats.

Actually, as far as the old myth goes, the Butter Cat got her name by being not a butter eater but a butter watcher. She was the farm's mouser and, in the house, the guardian of butter, milk, and cheese. As a result of her watchfulness—making sure no mice got any of these precious items—she was rewarded with a taste of any and all. From this well-tended and well-intended feline we get the image of the fat, or "well-buttered," cat.

Traditionally, the Butter Cat lay in the sunny windows of winter kitchens. But she was also given a special haven (usually in the bread warmer alcove) on, or very near, the stove.

A guardian against trolls, the Butter Cat was also considered to be the patroness of newlyweds and a blessing to the barn—not just because she caught mice. Her other attributes were good luck and bounty.

Remember, in our story, how Olaf and Sonja's luck seems to change when Sweet Butter comes to stay? This is a time-honored Nordic belief, for the goddess Freya, most powerful of all, had a cat-drawn chariot. Long after people forgot about Freya's greatness, they remembered those companion cats of hers.

Any hearth cat, then, became a symbol of wealth, well-being, and plenty of good butter.

THE SWORDSMAN AND THE CAT: A Japanese Zen Tale

There was once a famous swordsman named Ki who lived long ago in Japan. The steel of his sword was folded on the forge hundreds of times. In the end, the blade was so finely crafted that when the wind passed across it, the air was cut in two. The weapon had been in Ki's family for generations. The swordsman himself was so accomplished at kendo, the art of sword fighting, that no one would dream of entering his house uninvited.

However, there came a time when the swordsman was accosted by an intruder that he couldn't get rid of. The intruder was a large rat.

One day, the audacious rat ate soba noodles out of Ki's own enamel bowl.

"Remove yourself, rat!" Ki shouted. He then took his sword from the wall and, with perfect accuracy, brought it down on the rat.

However, when Ki raised his sword again, the rat was gone. The corner of the table was sliced like a piece of cheese. And there was the brazen rat— sucking a soba noodle over on the window ledge.

"My fine sword is too good for this annoying thief."

So, Ki emptied a vial of nightshade onto a rice cake and left it beside the hole where the rat lived. A few days later, the cake was still uneaten.

Next, Ki employed a cunning rattrap made of silk cord. Once into the trap's maze, the rat would not be able to get out. To Ki's amazement, however, the rat entered the trap, took the bait of cheese, and ate it on Ki's calligraphy table.

Although displeased by this turn of events, Ki was certainly not discouraged.

He purchased a slinky, black cat, who, it was said, ate a large rat every morning for breakfast.

"Mind this rat," Ki said to the cat, "for he is an exceptional foe."

The rangy feline lifted his head and smiled. The fur around his eyes showed some wear and tear, and one of the cat's ears had been gnawed at the tip.

"I see," said Ki, "that you are a warrior. Yet, I must tell you that what we have here is a martial arts master. This is a ninja rat. I am called the greatest swordsman in Japan, and yet I have no power over this impeccable fighter."

The black cat yawned and looked around the room.

Blinking his enormous spit-gray eyes, he slouched toward the rat's hole. He sniffed around it, flicking his tail.

Then Ki heard a munching noise. The rat appeared atop one of his favorite tomes, *The Book of the Sword.* He was eating the scarlet ribbon at the corner of the pressed-paper binding.

"Not my ancestors' great work," Ki said in chagrin.

Low-shouldered and quiet, the black cat assessed the necessary leap from the floor to the bookshelf. The rat looked on, a nearsighted expression on his fat face.

Suddenly, the crouching cat sprang.

Like a shadow, he flung himself to the shelf.

Landing precariously, he slid, clawing at books to regain his balance. The books tumbled and fell to the floor, as did the big black cat.

The rat, though, was nowhere to be seen.

Then, astonishingly, he appeared behind the cat and bit him on the tip of the tail. The cat cried. He whirled around to find the rat gone.

A moment later, the rat showed himself again.

This time, the black cat bowed and left the house of Ki forever.

As it happened, Ki, the greatest swordsman alive, was neither astonished nor dismayed. His years of training had taught him to keep his mind clear.

But now he summoned a cat trainer of great renown.

"I have a tabby so skilled in warfare with other animals that he is able to hunt dogs and hold them at bay. This miniature tiger will dispatch any rat on earth."

The price for the small tiger was a precious ancestor sword forged of ghostly steel. Ki was sad to part with it, but he was pleased to own the cat.

Now, as earlier, Ki spoke softly to the tabby, telling him what his adversary was like.

"This is no ordinary rat," he began, but the cat cut him short with a glance of his orange eye. He had one globular, oversized eye that was like a mismatched marble. The other eye, half its size, was sealed shut by a vicious scar. The big eye stared like a lamp. Never in his life had Ki encountered such a glare as this giant cat had. Even his own kendo master, long gone to the Golden Pavilion of Heaven, couldn't have locked eyes with such a martial cat.

"Very well," Ki assented, "I see that you are a staring master. Perhaps, in your previous life, you defeated the greatest of dharma warriors, those whose stare would turn opponents to stone."

The cat blinked disinterestedly.

So well did the rat understand the certainty of his power that he entered the room even while Ki was speaking.

At once, the cat turned his psychic stare on the rat.

Beady-eyed, the rat traded glances. But his were nervous and fleeting. Feebly, he squinted in that odd, nearsighted manner. All the while, the master tabby glared him down. The room got so hot, Ki opened his kimono to refresh himself.

Then, unexpectedly, the glowering cat lowered his face. The enormous eye closed, and the cat drooped like a wilted flower. His force spent, he bowed. And left the house of Ki forever.

Undeterred, Ki went to a traders' market. There he found a cat that fought cobras. This gray beast looked lackluster, but when facing a snake, he became a serpent himself.

"No snake can defeat my Gray," said the cat's owner. "You see how the cat drops back and seems to melt from view?"

"It is the same trick employed by my rat," Ki said.

The owner shrugged. "Watch how my cat kills the cobra with one bite."

Like a ground-hugging fog, the gray misty

cat faded away; like sudden smoke, he pounced. Afterward, the cobra lay dead.

"That is an enviable style," said Ki admiringly.

To own the animal, he was forced to give up the death sword of the great Chinese master Kung Li Shiu. This saddened him deeply, but he believed the trade was worth the loss.

Once he had brought the cat to his home, Ki spoke to him, introducing the invincible rat as was his custom. However, unlike the other cats, this one didn't listen at all.

"You don't understand," Ki said with concern. "This is no ordinary rat. You are an accomplished shadow fighter. That is also the style of the rat. Yet, he has been too quick and too confident for any of his opponents. You must recognize his authority before you meet the challenge."

The gray, though, had fought deadly snakes so long, he was not afraid of anything. While Ki spoke to him, the gray cleaned his paws. His green eyes were half-awake.

At this time, the rat entered the room. The gray ignored him, turning his back and dropping behind a red silk meditation cushion. Smokily he wafted away, leaving the rat sniffing the air and looking as nearsighted as ever.

Ki saw how the clever cat slipped under his tatami rug. He'd made himself small and inaccessible. The rat, for his part, strutted around the room in perfect nonchalance. Suddenly, from the rafters, it seemed, the gray fell upon the unsuspecting rat. But the rat threw him. Flattened by one well-timed throw, the humiliated cat conceded his defeat with a bow. Then he left the house of Ki forever.

Time passed, and Ki finally found an old temple cat. She was a mother, who was tired and lazy, and had no inclination to fight anymore. Ki discovered her at a local monastery, and the Zen master there agreed to hand her over for no payment at all, as was the tradition there. "She is a good mouser," the master said. "The best we've ever had."

Ki expressed his doubts. "She seems quite old."

"Don't let your eyes fool you. Age is no setback for those who are awakened."

Still, the unconcerned rat had

the run of Ki's home. Ki himself felt that he was no more than a guest.

The addition of the old temple cat meant nothing to the rat, who went about his business as usual. Day in and day out, the two ignored each other. The weary, bobtailed temple cat slept virtually all of the time. The rat ate whatever he pleased. Ki's house—and all the things in it—belonged to him now, and he had grown paunchy. He ate excessively.

And, what did he care about the old temple cat who slept all day on Ki's meditation pillow? She never lifted a paw against him—rarely, indeed, opened an eye to acknowledge his presence.

Naturally, the rat felt he owned the dozy cat.

Yet there came a morning when the rat hauled a smoked eel to his hole. Ki was planning to have the eel for dinner, but the rat had got to his larder first. Of course, there was no use trying to stop him, for he was too fast. However, as the rat scraped past the sleeping cat, she opened her eyes.

"Need some help?" she asked, yawning.

The idea had never entered the rat's mind, but now that he thought about it, he liked the notion of the cat doing his dirty work.

The rat, putting down the heavy eel, nodded.

"Glad to lend a hand," said the stiff, old bobtail.

Then, she sprang forward and, catching the rat entirely off guard, threw him to the floor.

Shamed by his defeat, the rat bowed and left the house of Ki forever.

"Yes," said Ki, who had seen saw the whole thing. He, too, bowed to the cat and remarked, "All my life I have developed a certain style of fighting, designed to cut down my enemy. But I have learned from you today that if you haven't an enemy, there is no need of a technique."

AFTERWORD

Cat magic is as popular in the mythology of the Far East as it is in Egyptian and European folklore. There are many legends of cats that assume human form, or of cats that behave exactly like people. In Asian tales the cat often takes the shape of an old woman, a priest, or a young girl. These sorcerers are abundant in Japanese folklore.

The famous temple cat is perhaps the best known of all breeds in Japan. Mythologically they are benefactors, felines who look after human beings and help guide them through life.

The Japanese temple cat has also been called the kimono cat because it is usually white with a so-called ink spot on its back. This artistic mark looks like a woman wearing a kimono, hence the name. Considered sacred, the cat is thought to possess the soul of an ancestor within it. Long ago, cats of this type were taken to a temple or monastery and left there for safekeeping.

Experts agree that the typical kimono cat is the Japanese bobtail, which looks like the Manx. If born with black, red, and white colors all over its body, the cat was called mi-ke, *or three-color. Always, this feline was considered to be a good-luck cat. Today, you can still find good-luck cat charms, statues, and amulets throughout Japan.*

In addition to the specific breed of cat discussed here, Japanese Zen monasteries often house cats of any color and disposition. They are left there because monks are generally kind and tolerant of cats. But also, perhaps, because of the old myth of the meditative, religious nature of the cat. The monks themselves laugh at this, however. They say that the cats keep down the mice, and that is why they are good to have around the monastery.

Spiegel and the Cat's Grease: A German-Swiss Legend

Do you believe that cats are wizards? Mysterious mistresses of long-forgotten secrets? White witches of the whirling void? Well, we believe that they are, and so do the storytellers in the Swiss Alps, who tell the tale of their famous Spiegel Katzchen.

He was a common cat, by the look of him. But as uncommon on the inside as he was common on the outside. For inside this particular *felix felidae,* or commonly uncommon cat, was the grease that makes mountains melt, treasures multiply, and waters rise and recede in the same sweeping motion as the mother sea herself.

Ah, Spiegel, ah, Katzchen.

Ah, magical, multifarious, nonnefarious, mystical cats of the world.

Well, anyway, there was once a certain wizard by the name of Gottfried. One day while he was out for his usual morning walk, he spied a ram cat. This old tom was walking along, remembering those better days, when he had been the favored feline of a rich gentlewoman whose sudden death had left him all alone in the world.

Gottfried, too, was down on his luck, for all of his recent spells had fallen short of their mark. His clients had stopped ringing his doorbell. He was feeling so low, in fact, at that very moment, he was thinking of ending his life. But, the sauntering, underfed cat caused Gottfried to reconsider.

He thought: *Look at the way that miserable excuse for a cat walks. Somehow, he manages to get along with more self-esteem than I, a master magician!*

"Katzchen," said the sad-eyed wizard to Spiegel, "where do you get your get-up-and-go?"

"My name is Spiegel, sir. Not Katzchen. And, as for that thing you call get-up-and-go . . . well, sir, that is just plain old cat's grease."

"Hmm. Cat's grease, you say?"

Gottfried knew about this magical infusion; wizards had used it for centuries. Its power came from the fact that it was hard to get, for only when a cat gave it voluntarily could a wizard use it for a spell.

Gottfried, seeing the poor cat's insufferable condition, had an idea. Eyes brightening, he twirled the tips of his huge walrus mustache. "Katzchen," said he, "I mean—Spiegel—won't you come to my house for lunch? I shall fatten you up and make you smile again."

Spiegel flicked his crooked tail. His battle-notched ears pricked up. His green marble eyes glowed. But, once a cat, always a cat, which means he was still cagey. What was this wizard up to? And why would he invite a poor cat to his table? "What are you having?" Spiegel asked warily.

"Baked mice," answered the wizard.

"What else?" said the testy cat.

"Why not wait and see what I set up for you," Gottfried said. He wiggled his fat sausage fingers. His black pig eyes burned. "I have things for you to see that no cat has ever seen before."

"Am I likely to see them again *after* I have eaten?"

"My dear Spiegel," Gottfried said softly. "Why are you so mistrustful? Had I known we would meet, I'd have built a castle in your honor. But as it is, we've just seen each other. Still, I plan to provide a feast that you'll never forget."

Spiegel's eyes became slitted as he considered this turn of events. "How about this afternoon?" he said indifferently.

"The very time I had in mind!"

"Now, what do you want, in return, from me?"

Spiegel knew one could never be too careful when in the presence of a wizard, especially one who was down on his luck. And this fellow, to be sure, had seen better days and more restful nights. Gottfried's ungroomed, grayish hair and his untidy clothes told a story no cat could overlook. He was, no doubt, a wizard out of work.

"I expect you to give me . . . " Gottfried pursed his pink lips and winked merrily. He paused, staring at the sky. "I shall expect some, just a little, maybe, just a tiny bit of—"

"Cat's grease," Spiegel finished.

Gottfried's eyes bugged out. This was a bargain made in heaven!

Now, Spiegel knew that cat's grease was cat's fat. To get some, you had to boil a cat down to its bare bones. Then, you had to throw away the bones and fur. What was left was cat's grease. Spiegel reasoned, *I don't have to worry about this bad-breath, fat, wheezy old wizard. Why, he couldn't cast a proper spell if his life depended on it.*

So Spiegel said, "Sure I'll fork over some grease. But you've got to feed me—and I mean *well.*"

"Consider it done, mein Katzchen, Spiegel."

The bargain between the man and the cat was fairly—and foolishly— struck, and later that afternoon, Spiegel showed up to collect his wages—the big feed. *I can always slip away from this half-crafty hippopotamus,* he thought, *but first I am going to eat like a king.*

Inside Gottfried's expansive house he had charmed a special world into being, just for his cat guest. He cast a respectable spell, and made a little mountain. Right next to it he conjured a little lake. In the trees, he cast small roasted pigeons. And all around the mountains he put baked mice, seasoned with stuffing and larded with bacon. What a conjuration he had performed! Fish swam in a diminutive lake that was white as milk—no, it *was* milk.

Spiegel, on seeing this, was overwhelmed. How could such a bumbleshoot magician do it? But he gave the trick no more thought, and he set upon the delicacies and ate them up. Whereupon, more appeared. And after that, still more.

The weeks went by, and then, the months. Spiegel, who had always planned on a speedy departure, had grown fat and lazy. It wasn't that he didn't want to leave; he *did*. But, somehow, he *couldn't*. So, he ate. In time, he was just too pudgy to budge.

One day, while Spiegel was nibbling on a candied trout, Gottfried looked down upon him eagerly. His lips were very wet, and his mustache was waxed and curled. *This is not the same ragged wizard who invited me in,* Spiegel thought.

True enough, Gottfried had also gone through a transformation. And, as Spiegel burgeoned, the wizard shrank. He had lost so much weight that he now wore natty clothes. He was well barbered, and his nails were clean and trim. Indeed, he looked the part of the successful spell-caster. "There is a small matter of some grease to be meted out, my roundish friend, Spiegel," said the magician.

Although Spiegel was fat and slow, his mind was still quick. "Sir," he said, "before you boil me up—or is it down?—I want to share my fortune with you."

"Where does an indigent cat get a fortune?" Gottfried scoffed.

"That's where you come in, sir," Spiegel chuckled. "For it will take a magician of your fame to get the golden bars I've been unable to retrieve, mine though they are."

"And where is this supposed fortune?"

"Deep in the bottom of a well. But first you must marry a penniless young woman at high noon. Same time, the gold becomes yours. Naturally, I, being a cat, couldn't accomplish such a feat."

Gottfried stroked his chin and gave his mustache a twirl. He knew that cats had lucky fortunes bestowed upon them. Everyone knew that. If the cat was lying, he would still exercise his other option—boiling Spiegel down to cat's butter, the grease that gave wizards their most gainful power.

On the other hand, the gold might be easy to get hold of. It might be as easy as one, two, and three.

"Shall we go to the well?" Spiegel asked.

Gottfried stroked his purple velvet cape with his open palm. "I believe we shall."

"I must say, I'd rather ride than waddle," Spiegel said.

"Then ride you shall," Gottfried announcd in his theatrical voice.

He flicked his cape from his shoulders and beckoned the cat to step upon it. Spiegel did so, and the magician followed suit. Gottfried commanded the cape to lift itself into the air. Then it rushed them in splendid silence over the forest trees and tiny hamlets and, at Spiegel's request, put them down exactly where the well was.

It lay in the basement of a ruined castle.

Immediately Gottfried peered into the hole. Spiegel sat at the wizard's feet. "Hmm, what you said was true. There *is* gold down there."

"Now, we must get to a young maiden," Spiegel reminded Gottfried. "The time is right," he added, "five of noon."

"And I'll be rich as a prince!" Gottfried chimed, clapping his hands.

"This is your lucky day," Spiegel added, "for I know a lady who will meet our requirement."

"Oh, fun!" said the happy wizard.

In more ways than one, Spiegel said to himself. For the young lady that he knew was really a witch. By day, a blond enchantress; by night, a hideous hag, who, whenever she wished, changed herself into a great gray owl.

So the cat and the wizard rode the purple cape to Spiegel's friend's house, high on the top of a mountain. A spindly tower it was, crookedly perched on the edge of a craggy abyss.

"A young maid lives in that cranky stone tower?" Gottfried was taken aback. The tower suggested another wizard. But as they floated past, a gorgeous blonde appeared in a window, smiling like a princess.

"Oh, my dear friend, Spiegel!" she cried. "Is it really you?"

"Indeed, it is. Can you come to the old well? We have need of you."

"I'll be there before you, precious puss!"

Said Gottfried, in surprise, "A lovely maid she is, sir."

Spiegel replied, "You'd lay down your life for her, if you weren't so set on gaining this gold."

"Be that as it may, we're two minutes away from twelve. Let's hasten to the marrying."

At the old well, the three positioned themselves—the beautiful maiden, whose name was Hilda; Spiegel, the clever cat; and Gottfried, the gold-struck wizard.

Forthwith, Spiegel married them, as was the ancient custom of good-luck cats.

Now, the deed was done. And so, too, did the gold rise from the deep, old well. One bullion bar at a time. Soon a mountain of them lay stacked like bricks in the afternoon sun.

"I could not have done this better if I'd done it myself," Gottfried said, smacking his lips. "What a day! I have a gorgeous wife, a fabulous fortune, and I'll still have my cat's grease, if you please."

"No problem, sir," said the smiling Spiegel. "Will you be greasing me here, or back at home, sir?"

"How about right here?" Gottfried twirled his mustache. Snapping his fingers, he conjured a cast-iron pot. Below it was a crackling fire. "In you go," Gottfried said. He squeezed Hilda's hand and laughed.

Spiegel began to step into the pot. When his left front foot was but a half inch from the boiling froth, Hilda heard him say something in Katschen-sprechen, or cat talk.

She understood what he said, though Gottfried did not.

Thus did she cast a spell that shrouded the sun. All at once, it was nightfall.

"How did that happen? I didn't order it." Gottfried, red in the face, began cracking his cape like a whip, trying madly to reverse the nighttime spell.

But instead the night grew darker.

"Sir," said Spiegel, chuckling, "meet my friend, Marta the owl."

Then Hilda changed into Marta, who flew into the sky and came soaring down with a soft, feathery hoot.

"That's nothing. I like owls—better than cats, anyway," the angry Gottfried retorted.

"Perhaps you will like Marta's sister, too." Spiegel laughed, and his belly shook. For there was Marta fully transformed into a gross, waxen witch. She cackled on the night wind.

She was, in fact, three things in one: a young woman, an owl, and a witch. Sometimes she could even be all three at the same time.

As Gottfried looked on in disgust, Marta the owl dusted her great, gray wings across the cold, gold fortune, and the bullion bars turned into bright trout that leaped back, one by one, into the old well.

When the last bar was gone, Gottfried sat on a mossy stone and begged his wife, "Would you at least remain lovely for me? I mean, we're married, aren't we? Why must you be an ugly witch, a crusty owl? I want Hilda the beautiful back."

"I don't think I'll be a human again for at least a thousand years," came Marta's voice trembling on the air. Then the night wind whined, and Marta called back, "I'll be waiting up for you, sweetie, after I've had my fill of mice."

Hearing how his fate was sealed, the luckless Gottfried danced round in rage, crying, "Fooled by a cat, cursed by an owl!"

Little did he know that once he'd married a witch, his powers were as good as gone. A broken man, he returned humbly to the tower of Marta to live the rest of his days in grief.

As for Spiegel, his powers increased. He had more cat's grease in him now than ever before, thanks to Gottfried feeding him all those candied trout and baked mice. Moreover, since the old magician's town house was now vacant, he took up residence there, and lived in luxury to a ripe old age.

And that is why all cats are said to possess magic, for, like Spiegel, they are clever beyond spells.

AFTERWORD

Cat magic, or the belief in it, has been distorted over the centuries into what is known as dark magic, or evil spells. Spiegel is not bad; he is good. So why is such an animal the companion of corrupt sorcerers? It's exactly as our story suggests: Good magic always wins in the end. Evil magic, sooner or later, gets the conjurer in trouble.

Cats have an inborn, nine-lived grace, which cannot be given to a human being without the cat's permission. Such feline myths exist throughout the world. The cat confers power when it's so disposed, never by command or through human malpractice.

The dark side of the tale is really the human part. Gottfried, the sorcerer, is wily and greedy—very human. He knows, in advance, that to obtain cat's grease he'll have to boil his cat, which means making a captive of him, fattening him up, and killing him. A dark quirk of human nature is our obsession with taking what doesn't belong to us—gold, grease, fame, fortune. For these can only be given, or earned, not stolen. So this wonderful German-Swiss fable is also an allegory, a tale of symbols with a special moral.

You might ask, as we do, what kind of cat Spiegel is. The answer—he's Anycat or Everycat. But because this story has its origin in the Swiss Alps, let's suppose Spiegel to be a European Shorthair. And let's further imagine him to be black, like the magic cats of the Middle Ages. The European Shorthair is a common breed, descended from the African wildcat, brought north by the Romans some two thousand years ago. In terms of quality, Spiegel and his kind are alert, active, ready mousers. They come in many colors—white, red, tortoiseshell, tabby, black, and all variations of these.

Incidentally, in case you were wondering if all cats have special curative or mystical qualities, we ought to mention that merely to stroke a cat in England was once a way of obtaining a touch of class, a whisper of immortality, or even a bag or two of riches.

The Goddess Cat

Bast, the Cat Goddess: An Ancient Egyptian Myth

One morning, Ra, the hawk-headed god of the sun, saw his cat-faced wife, Bast, sleeping on a cloud. Bringing his chariot to a stop on a cloud-cliff nearby, he got out and walked to where she was blanketed in fire-gold fleece.

"The earth people have erected another statue of you, my dear. It is along the Nile. A good likeness, I think. Have you seen it?"

Bast stroked her whiskers lightly with her fingertips. The earth people pleased her with their faithful worship. However, she knew their love of fighting, their love of blood. "Do you see those armies amassing around Pelusium, the sacred city of the Egyptians?"

Ra flashed a hawk's look at the desert sand below. "I see them. They're Persians, are they not?"

"Indeed," she replied, "they are. And they come to vanquish our subjects, those we've vowed these many hundred years to protect."

Ra had no spirit left to intervene. Every night he fought Apep, the Serpent of Darkness; and defeating him, Ra was responsible for the rising sun. This was his greatest service to mortals. Once, when he was younger, he had taken the magic Eye out of his belt and cast it down upon the human race to teach them a lesson. They were arrogant, war-making fools, and he wished to stop their silliness, once and for all.

"I remember well," Bast said, stretching, "when you cast your magic Eye, and the desert sand turned to flame. It swept over the armies of men and devoured them." She looked at him accusingly. "You made men from your tears. Yet, when they fought against one another, you became short-tempered with them and almost vanished them from the earth."

Ra took up a handful of glittery cloud sand, letting the rainbowed granules filter through his palm. The crest feathers of his hawk's headdress rose and fell. "I suppose, when all's said and done, we're no different from mortals, my precious. They've got our precarious moods and dispositions, do they not?"

Bast smiled a thin, cat-whiskered smile. She was woman, from her toes to her neck. However, her beautiful head was all cat. Her tall, tapered ears stood upright. Her sapphire eyes gleamed. "We cannot allow the Persians to kill the children of the Pharaohs."

"If they did that, the beautiful temples of Bast would fall," Ra said sadly.

"I'll have to attend to *this* battle myself," Bast said with determination.

"I am no stranger to the collapse of worlds, to conquerors and conquests, to the end of dynasties," spoke Ra. "The reason I once unleashed my fury on mortal men and women was that they seemed never to have enough bloodshed. Always, war, war, war."

From the clouds where they stood, the two gods looked into the magic Eye that Ra took from his golden belt. It was shaped like a diamond, sharp at the ends.

As they peered into it they saw the smoky desert plains where mortal armies fought one another. The clash of armor and the whine of arrows were audible even from so great a height, for the magic Eye conveyed everything to them.

"What should I do?" Bast wondered.

"Look into the Eye," Ra answered. "All solutions lie therein. The past, the future."

"I want to see the future."

"So," he answered, "it is done."

As Bast glanced now into the Eye, she saw something new. This time a great, dark shape rose over the horizon and engulfed the bloody battlefield. It seemed to be made of fur and it flowed like water. It made a humming, drumming sound, like that of the sistrum, or tambourine, she carried with her at all times. The Eye showed that this thing, this strange, sand-shifting, fur-gliding shape with its vibrating sound, had won the day. For the Persian army was laying down its arms. So, she saw in surprise, were the Egyptian forces. The battle was done.

The Eye clouded, closed. Ra put it back into his gilded belt.

Gem-eyed Bast smiled. Now she understood the future. And recognized what she must do. "I hadn't thought of that," she said in wonder. "Thank you, Ra."

Ra grinned. His old face lit anew.

At once, Bast began to shake her sistrum. The sand-swept land vibrated with the jingling sound. The earth seemed to hear the heavenly noise.

Cat-headed Bast floated down, strumming her celestial instrument. Drifting invisibly above the fields where the fighting raged, she made her song louder than the clash of iron and bronze, stone and steel. Armed men, locked in mortal combat, heard the sistrum's music, and stopped.

Bast surveyed the fighting field and spied the one she wanted, the lone man to carry out her divine plan.

"What is that noise?" said Cambyses, the leader of the Persian army—he whom Bast had chosen. He had been pitted against a sea of Egyptian warriors, but all had paused, listening.

The tense, feline air was whiskered with magic. Everyone heard it, but Cambyses felt it as no other. "Lay down your arms," he cried. "Stop fighting at once!"

His men began to retreat, walking backward to their camp. Mystified, the Egyptian soldiers stared in surprise as the Persians faded from sight.

After returning to his encampment, Cambyses said to his men, "Do not lose heart. We've been given a divine omen. Did you not hear the sound of the heavens speaking to us?"

"We heard," said one of his soldiers, "but what would you have us do?"

Cambyses smiled. "I want you to find all the cats that live in this place. We are going to take them on a grand march into the city, which shall be opened to us without further fighting."

"What strange things you say!" muttered the captain of the guard, who

wondered what this would lead to. "Have you gone mad, Cambyses? Cats are not weapons."

High overhead, a golden hawk cried crisply on the wind. It sounded, in fact, like a cat's mew.

Cambyses looked at the sky. In his ears alone, now, the purring continued. It hummed like the beat of his blood.

"Signs," he cried. "More signs!"

Cambyses, a legend in his own time, was not one to take messages, or omens, lightly. Nor were his soldiers about to disobey their leader. If he said to stop fighting and gather cats, they would do that thing.

So the Persians searched the desert dunes for eight days and eight nights, seizing every cat they could find. Nor did they have far to look, for legions of cats were everywhere.

Gold and gray, spotted and cream, misted and molten, they came—in such numbers and on so many padded feet that the sand was scored with the hieroglyphic imprints of their paws.

When all the cats were rounded up and each soldier had a cat in arm, the warriors again returned to the battlefield. Yet this time, aside from their feline friends, they were unarmed.

The Egyptians stared from their stronghold, the great white sun city of Pelusium. Prepared for attack, they drew a deep breath when they witnessed what was coming. Across the sand marched the unarmed men. And with them, an armada of so many cats, they couldn't be counted.

The men cradled them in their arms, as Cambyses had said to do. But many cats, of their own volition, crept ahead of the advancing Persian forces. The sand dunes appeared to shrink in the swell of the amassing cats. By the thousands they furled and unfurled their tails.

And kept on coming, a slow tide of amber fur.

Behind them followed the Persians—with Cambyses himself holding his own cat upon his head.

The sand had turned into a great Nile of flowing fur, and the dry air buzzed now with an insistent purr like the stringed notes of the sistrum, the cat-headed Egyptian tambourine.

Transfixed, the Egyptian army held their ground, but their hands fell uselessly to their sides. Weapons dropped, clanged.

Everyone knew that the punishment for killing a cat was death. Cats were sacred, and as these precious animals made their way toward the gates of the city, the Egyptian soldiers laid down their arms and surrendered.

Into the city of Pelusium streamed the thousands of cats; behind them came the peaceful Persian conquerors.

That night the wine flowed. The Egyptians and the Persians celebrated the end of their war, and they toasted one another in peaceful communion. They could not do otherwise, for the cats' eyes were on them. Wherever men and women gathered, the cats sat in judgment of them. Bast herself had no need to be present; the cats were there in her stead.

It was for this reason the war was over and two separate people were joined. In truth, the cats ruled.

And, once again, when the sun rose the next morning, the people knew that Ra had defeated Apep, the Serpent of Darkness.

Bast was with him, and the people, Persians and Egyptians alike, placed flowers at the feet of her statue on the Nile.

On high and looking into his magic Eye, Ra sighed with pleasure. "I may have vanquished Apep, but you, my dear, have lifted darkness from the hearts of men."

Bast smiled, and her lips turned up at the corners, the way cats smile to this day.

AFTERWORD

The quintessential Egyptian cat, from which all others may be said to stem, is the Mau. Cats that approximate her are visible in Egyptian art from 1400 B.C. The Abyssinian is virtually the same feline, but the Mau is generally thought to be the cat worshiped at Bubastis along the Nile.

In fact, both breeds have sleek forms, narrow shoulders, tapered tails. They each have triangular heads, short noses, and large almond eyes. Therefore, either cat could be the one that you see on papyrus and bronze.

The name Mau means "cat" in ancient Egyptian. The so-called M on the face of this feline is said to be a Mau line. In any case, these markings were so much in fashion that Egyptian women imitated them by using kohl, as eyeliner, to accent their own eyes. They therefore created special accents to give their faces a feline look.

The idea of being two-faced also comes from the Egyptian cat concept. It was a compliment. If you had two faces, you also had two natures, double power, instead of singular. This made you more potent. Accordingly, Bast had two sides. Her destructive personality was Sehkmet, the ruthless cat goddess. Her nurturing self was Bast, the kindly cat deity.

As we know, the cats of ancient Egypt were not only revered; they were worshiped. The actual battle account of the Persians in the year 500 B.C. is fully recorded. When they laid siege to Pelusium (called Tisseh, near Port Said, Egypt), the city fell without a blow. The cat defense ploy, as we've described it, worked perfectly.

There is also the story of the Greek general Galsthelos, who commanded Pharaoh's army and was defeated at the parting of the Red Sea. He lived to see another day, though, as he escaped with his wife, Scota, the Pharaoh's daughter. Eventually, the general came to Portugal and settled there, but some centuries later a member of his family left Portugal and founded a country far to the north. This man named his north land after his ancestor, the beautiful Scota, and he called the country Scotland. For its mascot he selected a cat, which was a relative of the Egyptian Mau.

The Monster Cat

The Tale of the Whittle Cat: A Middle European Myth

Once there was a cat that liked to eat. It was, in fact, a gorging puss, an animal remembered in Europe even today. There are many names for this feline. It's been called the gorging cat, the carving cat, the fat cat, the whittle cat.

And some call it the monster cat.

Long before you were born, there was a woodcutter and his wife who lived on the edge of a great forest. They had no children, and this made them very lonely. Not the husband so much as the wife. He, it seemed, was content living so far from others.

Every morning the woodcutter's wife said, "Oh, how I wish I had a child to take care of. All day you are gone to the woods, felling trees. I am here alone, wishing there was a baby to cuddle."

The woodcutter would reply, "When I come home from work, you can take care of me."

He wasn't a mean man, but he was tired of hearing his wife's complaint. Moreover, they weren't young people, either of them, so there was no point in wishing for what they couldn't have.

One afternoon the woodcutter was gathering mushrooms in the forest when he saw something that caught his eye.

A pine knot was growing out of the trunk of a tree, and the more the man looked at it, the more certain he was that this thing was the answer to his wife's loneliness.

This pine knot had the face of a cat. The woodcutter took out his knife and loosened the knot. He then sat down and carved the bark off it.

"What a wonderful little wooden kitten." The man chuckled. Pink and clean, the knot was the exact replica of a baby cat minus the fur.

When he was done whittling, the woodcutter put the shapely pine knot in his lunch pail and took it home to his wife. At the door of their cottage, she greeted him with her sad face.

He said, "Look at the piece of wood I found in the forest while I was gathering mushrooms." Proudly, he showed off the whittle cat.

"Where are the mushrooms?" demanded his wife, not looking at his gift.

"Oh, I forgot all about them," he answered, "after I saw this beautiful thing." Again, he offered his wife the whittle cat.

It was clean and nice, and he'd whittled it smooth so that it really resembled a cat with its mouth wide open, as if hoping for something to eat.

The wife regarded the cat carefully. The look on her face was skeptical but slightly amused. She turned the cat round and round. "Maybe . . . ," she mused, her face flickering with a passing fancy. The wrinkles around her eyes and mouth suddenly seemed to vanish. Then she grew solemn and still. "Husband," she advised, "this isn't a piece of wood."

"Well," he said, fumbling with his rough hands, "it does look like—"

But before he could finish, his wife dismissed him with a brush of the hand. "Don't you have something to do before I set out your supper?" She was eyeing the whittle cat with admiration, and beginning to cradle it in her arms.

Relieved, the woodcutter smiled and sat down on a stool by the fireplace. "I see that you like my little toy," he said, his ruddy cheeks flushed with joy. He'd never seen his wife so animated. Now she was stroking the whittle cat, rubbing her hand along its spine as if she expected the tail to wiggle.

"What a splendid cat!" she cried emphatically.

After supper the woodcutter and his wife sat at their table and drank a small glass of cherry kirsch.

The wife polished off hers with one swallow. Wiping her mouth on the corner of her apron, she cocked her head to one side like a happy wren.

"You know," she said sweetly, "although I've always wished for a child, this whittle cat may be the very thing I longed for." She studied the taut, closed-eyed kitten in her lap. The carving was so well done that the thing seemed to possess a life all its own. Again and again, the wife ran her hand down its back with smooth satisfaction.

The woodcutter's Adam's apple bobbed once as he finished off the colorless white liquor. His eyes were questioning as he asked, "But is it really enough?"

"Husband," whispered the wife, "I never dreamed that such a thing could be so wonderful. All at once, I feel so young again." Her cheeks burned with an autumn glow, and her eyes looked winsomely at the whittle cat, which she cradled lovingly in her arms.

"Well," he said, "at least it's ours. Finally, you have what you've always wanted, and you won't be lonely anymore when I leave you to go cut wood."

As time went on, the woodcutter's wife began to feed the whittle cat the same food that she and her husband ate at the table. If they ate dumplings, so did the cat. If they were having sausage, the wife fed the whittle cat so tenderly, just as if it were a child. Well, of course, she didn't really expect the wooden cat to eat these things, but she playfully pretended that it was so, and her husband overlooked this eccentricity with an amused smile. *What does it matter, as long as she is happy?* he thought to himself.

Once, she fed it some corn porridge, with milk and sugar, and this wet gruel dribbled down the whittle cat's carved mouth and onto the plank floor. Neither the wife nor her husband paid any attention to this, however.

Always, now, her face glowed with expectancy and love. He, for his part, shrugged at her antics with the cat, but he enjoyed the little pecks on the cheek she kept giving him. All in all, they were most happy; happier than they'd been in years.

So, for some weeks thereafter, the whittle cat behaved exactly as you would expect a piece of wood to act—lifelessly. But one morning, while feeding it a breakfast of blackberries, the wife gave a little start as the whittle cat leaped out of her lap. It struck the floor solidly with all four hard wood paws.

"Get me some meat!" it ordered in a mealy, squealy voice.

The woodcutter fell off his stool, he was so amazed.

His wife, though, didn't blink. "Oh, how our whittle cat can talk," she cooed.

"Cats don't speak," said the woodcutter flatly. "Neither do pieces of wood!"

"Ah, but ours does!" the wife retorted calmly.

"Well, I've never seen any such thing," the woodcutter muttered.

"Go out to the smokehouse and get a leg of venison," she said.

Numbly, the woodcutter did this, wondering what was happening, and where it would end.

That night, the wife cooked a bubbling venison stew, and she fed some to the whittle cat, who actually ate it, grabbing at each morsel like a snapping turtle. First, she fed him with a wooden spoon. But the whittle cat, biting down on a chunk of meat, growled and clawed the spoon out of the poor woman's hand. Then he put his paw into the stew pot, which was on the table, and ripped out the best chunk of venison. Thereupon, the famished whittle cat picked up the black pot and poured the hot stew into his wide, white, open mouth.

"Can't you see he needs more meat!" the wife yelled at her husband. Meekly, the stunned woodcutter got to his feet and went out to the smokehouse. "Where will this lead to?" he asked himself as he cut a generous and choice steak from the hanging carcass. He had misgivings about what was happening, and yet he knew he himself was somehow responsible. He was the one who had whittled the cat out of a pine knot.

The moment the whittle cat eyed the red meat, he pounced on it, tearing the flesh and crunching the bones. After which, he said hoarsely, "More meat!"

Now, the way it happened, the crazed whittle cat never stopped eating. After he'd eaten up all the meat that was stored away in the smokehouse, he staggered outside into the yard. His belly bulged and dragged. The rest of him, however, was just as scrawny as ever. In fact, the veins of his skin were no more than grains in the wood of a juniper tree. He looked wooden yet he moved like a living thing, a creature of flesh and bone, sinew and claw. And his sap-filled eyes glowed like lamps.

The whittle cat went out into the yard and caught the woodcutter's pigs, eating them on the spot. This still wasn't enough sustenance for him, so he gobbled down a flock of geese and a couple of milk cows. In addition, he devoured some goats, one by one, as they hopped over the fence, and into his mouth—and, all the while, the whittle cat grew larger. And larger. Time passed; days went by. The whittle cat got immense, towering above his benefactors.

Soon he was so big that he couldn't fit into their cottage at all. He was bursting at the seams—or, rather, grains—but he couldn't control his craving for meat, and he kept on gorging. Going from farm to farm and house to house, he ate whatever came his way—wild, domestic, it didn't matter.

There was a herd of draft horses, belonging to a farmer who was always pulling out pine stumps to increase his fields. Into the whittle cat's cavernous jaws went those huge, ponderous horses, one after the other. Afterward, the whittle cat's stomach made a furrow in the earth as it dragged, but still, he wasn't satisfied; still, he was hungry.

The woodcutter and his wife didn't know what to do. So they did nothing.

"I think he's outgrown us," the wife said to her husband after the whittle cat had left them. They'd always been poor, but now they were poorer, for the whittle cat had eaten everything. "But it's so sad to see him leave us," said the wife, weeping.

The woodcutter just scratched his head. "The farmers in the valley are mad at us," he said. "They say we must pay for the loss of their livestock."

"Whoever would've thought," she said, shaking her head.

Now, the whittle cat was about as big as a barn when he left them, sniffing the ground for traces of food. There was nothing in the immediate countryside to eat, so he started eating trees. Soon he'd polished off a whole forest. After that he gorged himself on hills, valleys, headlands, marshes, fields, houses, barns, and, ever on the move, he finally jumped into the sky and ripped off a hunk of the moon. That made him feel sick, but it didn't stop him from nibbling the sun the next morning. However, the sun was much too hot, and he spat it out and then he began to choke.

He'd caught hold of some fiery rays, and they were burning up his pitchy, wooden throat. Presently, the whittle cat's head burst into flame. Then all that was left of him was his prodigious belly. Bulbous and smooth, it filled a whole field like an enormous melon. Then, this, too, burst open, and out came all the things that the whittle cat had eaten.

One at a time, they walked, rolled, tumbled, and fell out into the light of day. There were goats, geese, horses, cows, trees, wagons, carts, houses, barns, and all manner of things, including a church and its steeple, and even a river barge. Hills, marshes, and forests also oozed and flowed out into the topsy-turvy air.

And all of these went back to their place of origin, as if nothing strange had ever happened to them.

Now, the woodcutter and his wife heard of this and they breathed a sigh of relief. The wife no longer wept over the loss of her loved one, nor did she wish for his return.

The woodcutter said, "It didn't turn out the way we wanted, but at least we don't owe anyone any money."

The wife replied, "I suppose we're better off this way—not having such a large mouth to feed all the time." Yet there was something wistful and sad in her tone.

"Well," the husband said. "You know, all I ever wanted was for you to be happy."

The woodcutter's wife nodded. "We have each other," she responded. She winked at him as he sat there by the fire, warming his hard, callused hands.

He winked back. Things returned to normal for the two of them, and the wife no longer said, "Oh, how I wish we had a child!"

However, she now had such a fondness for cats that there were always a number of them hanging around the cottage crying for milk. A few got to be quite fat, but they never said anything except *meow*.

AFTERWORD

The myth of the gorging cat comes from many countries. In Scandinavia, this unmanageable creature devours a husband and wife known as Goodman and Goody, then he goes on to swallow a bunch of animals, a wedding party, a funeral train, and finally, the sun and the moon. After which, as we know, he disgorges all of them, intact.

The Celtic "cat a' leasa" is a fearsome creature, dragonlike and dangerous. In Ireland, he is still known as Kate Kearney's Cat. Oldest of all things, he goes so far as to eat the calendar year, thus consuming time itself.

The truth is, this is a universal story. Every country seems to have one, and all seem to love theirs equally. Native Americans once described the gorging creature as a huge serpent, something like the Egyptian Lord of Darkness, Apep. In fact, some mythologists believe this motif comes from the ancient Egyptian belief in "the cat that swallows the serpent that was trying to strangle the sun."

Naturally the gorging-cat theme can reflect any breed at all. The whittle cat is just your common alley variety, otherwise known as the household pet.

The Guardian Cat

The Temple Cat of Lao-Tsun: A Southeast Asian Myth

In the desert region of Burma there lived long ago a sacred cat. It lived in the underground Temple of Lao-Tsun. This legendary cat guarded the holy Lama, Mun-ha, the most honored of all men in that country.

In his remote monastery of stone, which was carved to look like a giant cat, Mun-ha lived in secrecy. Behind the cat-pawed arches that formed the gateway of the palace he sat upon a throne with golden, lion-footed armrests. Beside him there was a smaller, yet identical, seat for his sacred cat, Sinh. Otherwise the room was bare.

Actually, Sinh the cat was the ruler of the kingdom. According to legend, he advised Mun-ha by sending him telepathic thoughts. Thereafter, when the Lama voiced them, they became law.

One day, however, the kingdom was attacked by an army of Brahmin warriors from nearby India. Finding a way through the barrier of intricate walls and labyrinths, they discovered the hidden gateway to the secret hermitage of Mun-ha. Before them rose a giant stone cat, whose open mouth had a door in it and whose eyes were enormous sapphires. Below them the cat's great paws rested on the sandy ground. Here was the South Door of Mun-ha's residence, unopened and unviolated by strangers.

The two kingdoms of India and Burma had been at war for centuries, but now, as the Brahmins lit their camphor torches and notched their bows, the siege against Mun-ha began.

Even before the Brahmins had taken their first step, however, Sinh saw them in a vision.

Stroking his long yellow beard, Mun-ha received Sinh's message. "But who is it that comes to the South Door?" he asked the cat.

The gilt eyes of Sinh slowly closed. *I see our enemies, the Brahmins.*

Mun-ha shivered as he straightened his foot-long beard. "Will they kill me?" he wanted to know.

They will try to.

Mun-ha accepted these words with poise. "Well, what are we to do?"

Already, however, the incense sticks of jasmine were vibrating on their trays of gold. Their smoke was being drawn toward the South Door of the palace, as if to the calamity that was about to unfold.

As always, the cream-colored cat replied, *we will remain unmoved by violence. The Brahmin warriors shall not penetrate this holy chamber.*

Mun-ha was surprised. His fine, thin eyebrows uplifted. "Then how," he questioned, "can they hurt me?"

By their nearness to your holiness.

Mun-ha drew a deep breath, which he released as if pouring a cup of tea and not wanting it to spill. The master's silk coat, embroidered with butterfly patterns, touched the floor. He knew that his time had come. Soon, he'd be reborn in another world.

At the South Door, the Brahmin warriors began their attack. Their hand axes sank into the teak wood. The honed blades fell at intervals, reddish wood chips flailing. Within the temple the blows sounded distant, as if the primordial heart of the mountains were beating.

"My spirit weakens," Mun-ha whispered. He fingered his beard, glancing into the topaz eyes of Sinh. "What is happening?" he asked.

The cream cat listened. His folded paws were smudged with brown, as were the tip of his tail and his nose. He was altogether lovely and completely composed. *Do not fear,* Sinh said, *I will be with you on your journey.*

Mun-ha lowered his head. He was meditating.

Outside in the high desert glare, the sun pounded on the shaved heads of the Brahmin men. Their bright axes arced and fell sharply. The great door quaked—a shaft of sunlight pierced the supernal darkness of the Temple of Lao-Tsun.

More axes sank into the teak; the door fell with a crash.

At the same time, Mun-ha's eyelids fluttered. His head rested back; he released a deep sigh, the sound of which filled the empty throne room. All but one of the camphor lamps smoked out. Mun-ha was dead.

Then from five inner courtyards, long lines of gold-robed priests came into the throne room of Mun-ha. Intuitively they knew that their master was gone. Yet, without fear, they settled to the floor, assuming the lotus position. There was no violence in them. They heard the South Door being breached; they made no move to stop it.

The throne room of Mun-ha was very still except for the noise of the Brahmins. The angry bite of the axes stopped, but the voices of swordsmen were heard within.

The seated priests sat, their eyes half-closed.

Now Sinh leaped onto the head of his master. He landed, soft as a leaf.

Master, said the cat, *the intruders shall never touch you.*

The master, though dead, appeared to nod.

Every priest saw it. Each made a mudra, a sacred gesture of the hands.

The footfalls in the hall grew louder.

Fear not, said the cat, to all present.

The trace of a smile seemed to awaken the lips of the departed Mun-ha. Was he—alive?

His eyes fluttered open.

The robed monks now witnessed the unfolding of a miracle!

They saw Sinh's fur change from cream to white gold. Exactly the same color as the master's hair and beard. Too, the cat's topaz eyes turned to azure blue. His dusky paws whitened and were gold-tinged wherever they touched Mun-ha's head.

Again, the monks made a mudra with their hands. Yet no one said a word.

61

The wisest of the monks smiled. "Mun-ha's soul is within the sacred cat."

"All is well," said a round of voices.

Then every robed man bowed toward Mun-ha. But the master didn't move; it was the sacred cat who blinked his turquoise eyes.

After this, Mun-ha and Sinh vanished.

So did the footfalls of the intruders, the warriors themselves fading away into the mountain passes. No explanation has ever been given for their mystic retreat. The enemies of the Temple of Lao-Tsun left, never to return.

It is said that Sinh carried his master's soul to heaven on that very day. Neither one has returned, but the Temple has been ruled by cats ever since that time. They are clothed in gold and gloved in white, and always they resemble Sinh. When a new Lama is chosen to rule over the Temple, one of the sacred cats makes this selection—for, they say, no human being has the wisdom to do so.

AFTERWORD

The sacred cat in our tale is the Southeast Asian feline known as the Birman. In the beginning of the story, the cat sounds like a Burmese, for it has this breed's traditional gold eyes. But as our story concludes, the breed changes, as do the eyes—from gold to azure blue, with the coat changing from cream to white gold.

The Birman is known to have lived in the holy temples of Burma, under the protection of the Lama. However, it is also clear that the Lama lived under the protective eyes of the cat, too. And his future lives depended upon the grace and godliness of this feline, who would become the repository of his soul.

The myth told here is like a lot of Asian cat tales in that it shows what an ancestor cat really is. This is a cat that guards the body and soul of a human being. When that person passes on, physically, the cat draws in and holds the essence, or soul, of that individual. In time, as our tale suggests, the cat releases the person's soul and takes it to heaven. Therefore, the white-gold, cloud-reflected light of the cat is magical, unearthly.

The legendary Birman certainly fits the bill. Hoary-furred and regal, china-blue-eyed, white-gloved and -booted—it's a kind of dream cat. Silkier than the Persian, the Birman is a shimmering cloud of fluff. Its enigmatic face is wonderfully wise. Its points—muzzle, ears, and tail—are sooty-looking. The cat's famous gloves and boots are whitish yellow. Overall, it's a stunning creature, who is as happy indoors as it is outdoors, thus, a living definition of the Buddhist nature.

Kit Cat of Cat Key: A Bahamian Legend

There was once a pirate named Calico Jack, whose real name was Jack Rackham. Some claimed he was a black-hearted man, whose cruelty caused his untimely death by hanging in Port Royal, Jamaica. But there were others who knew him, and they said Jack had a heart of gold, especially when it came to mermaids and calico cats. There was an abundance of each in the Bahama Banks when Jack started out as a cabin boy back in 1709.

This tale is about one particular calico cat, however; a good-luck ship's cat named Kit Cat. At that time every ship had its cat: not for decoration, but because it was thought to be the best guardian against bad weather.

One day when Jack was coiling rope on the bow of a Bahamian square-rigger, he chanced to look across the deck. Out in the bright light he saw a school of dolphins. They were singing and sporting along the bow.

As soon as Jack saw them, he had an idea—an inglorious one, we might add—but that was the way Jack was before Kit Cat taught him a lesson he "never remembered," as he himself was fond of saying.

Jack took a harpoon and made ready to strike. Now, everyone knows it's bad luck to kill a dolphin, but Jack cared nothing for superstition. He cared only for Jack.

So he might have done that dirty deed had it not been for Kit Cat, that big, splotchy, orange-and-black calico kitty who decided to change the course of Jack's life.

Just as Jack was ready to throw his harpoon, Kit Cat jumped on his back.

Zrrrt!—Kit Cat's claws caught the furl of Jack's loose cotton shirt. Then, *booey*, both of them went over the bowsprit into a blizzard of bubbles. And each was gone before you could say, "The wind's made a wicket of the captain's beard."

As the foamy brine closed over Jack's head, something flashed under him, a dark shadow of the bluey deep. It wasn't Kit Cat, for she was swimming above his head. It was the very dolphin Jack had been aiming at, but he didn't know it. Dolphins and sharks look much the same when you're struggling in the sea. However, this dolphin was trying to save his life. But no one on the ship seemed to notice that Jack and Kit Cat were down in the drink.

Now, as the dolphin chittered and circled him, Jack made it to the surface. What was the dolphin saying? Only Kit Cat knew, for cats and dolphins understand each other's language.

When Kit Cat climbed onto the dolphin's back, Jack did the same, throwing one leg over each side, as if he were riding a horse. As soon as they were safely on, the dolphin took them for the ride of their lives. Through the glitter she cruised, the cerulean swells parting as she carved them with her bottle-shaped nose.

In the distance the ship was shadowing the horizon, disappearing beyond sight.

Now it seemed to Jack that the dolphin was taking them to the Riding Rocks—an escarpment of spray-lashed pinnacles near the upper end of Cat Key, the Bahamian Island where Kit Cat had been born. The Riding Rocks were given that name by stranded sailors who were thankful to be there. For days and weeks a man might cling to these two projectiles of sea-chiseled rock, waiting—sometimes in vain—for rescue.

And this was where the dolphin dropped them off. And where, without so much as a by-your-leave, she departed.

"Well, here we are," Jack said, "half-drowned and wholly hopeless."

"Don't be so down in the mouth," Kit Cat said, licking the salt off her tail.

"You . . . talk?"

"All cats talk—if it pleases them."

Jack whistled through his teeth. "Don't that beat all—rescued by a fish that I tried to kill and here I am talking with a cat!"

Kit Cat, yellow fur plastered to her frame, looked as flat as a flounder.

"Okay, talking puss, tell me what our chances be."

Kit Cat climbed to the top of the Riding Rocks, where the air was spiked with sunlit spray. Forepaws on the topmost rock, she scanned the bleary horizon. "Our best hope is to call for help," she told Jack.

He blinked beyond the glare, saw nothing. *Help?* he wondered. *From whom?*

Kit Cat began to sing, "Oo-la-loo, oo-la-loo."

"Cats can sing?" Jack said, surprised.

Kit Cat answered, "What cats cannot do hasn't been done." And as Kit Cat sang again, a round head appeared between the breakers.

"Oo-la-loo," Kit Cat yodeled.

The head of a girl surfaced, then vanished.

"She's come to rescue us," Kit Cat said to Jack.

Jack pinched himself. *Dreaming, am I? A talking cat and a bobbing sea lass. I must be dreaming.*

The green-gold head gleamed in the rolling window of waves. Kit Cat purred, "She awaits a kindness, Master Jack. Can you not show the creatures of the sea the goodness that is in all men? Even yourself."

"I be not a man, Kit Cat. But something other—pirate, perhaps."

"Then be a pirate of goodly nature," she said, licking her salt-wet bib.

Jack sighed. "If we're rescued, truly I'll mend my ways."

"You must promise me on a stack of Bibles to treat the finned people of the sea and the four-legged people of the land as you would want to be treated yourself."

Jack smiled. "All right, then. If it must be, it must be. I vow to look at the world with a brand-new looking glass."

Kit Cat grinned. The girl's head shone above the waves.

Jack called to her, "We'll not hurt you." But his voice didn't sound sincere.

"How could you?" came the salty reply.

Kit Cat batted Jack's cheek with her paw. "Try harder, Jack. This time, be polite—and mean it."

"I meant what I said before," he said resentfully.

"That wasn't how it sounded."

"My dear young lady," Jack began as he saw the girl's head appear over the swell.

"I'm much older than you—"

"Well, I cannot very well say, 'My dear old lady,'" Jack said.

The mer-girl nodded. This time she smiled. The foam and weed washed about her as she held herself afloat.

"What do you call yourself?" Jack asked.

"Your cat knows my name."

"Oolaloo is her name," said Kit Cat. "Did you think I was saying it just for fun?"

The mer-girl smiled again and disappeared behind a huge wave.

Jack was asking Kit Cat, "But how is any of this blinkety-blankety talk going to fetch us off the rock?" when Oolaloo resurfaced. Her throat was necklaced with bright little bubbles. Her pretty face was the dark of brown honey, and she had very sharp teeth like those of a fish. Otherwise, she was lovelier than the loveliest of land girls.

"You've a capital name," Jack said.

"And what is yours, if I may ask?"

"They call me Calico Jack because of my trousers."

"If you lived with us, you wouldn't have need of them."

"Would that we could," Jack said.

"I'll show you how nice our world is if you promise me that you're a changed man. No more harpoons?"

"Aye," Jack spoke. "I don't favor them anymore. But is it all right to eat a little fish now and then?"

"We do," she answered. "But only what's necessary to live. So, do you wish to come with me now? Let me take you to my home, where all the mer-folk live in peace with one another. After you've seen it, I'll return you to your ship."

"I'm willing," Jack said.

Then, at the mer-girl's beckoning, they jumped off the Riding Rocks into the wide swell of the sea and they followed her sparkling silver bubbles into greeny gloom. Jack opened his eyes and saw a lilting, tilting world. His fingertips touched the outspread fin of the mer-girl, and thus was he propelled along. Kit Cat sank her claws into Jack's calico cuff and followed. They held their breath, and as long as Jack maintained his finger-tipped

touch of the mer-girl, he and Kit Cat had no further
need of air.

Now the white-riffled sea floor was just below them.
They passed through ribs of ancient ships. Canyons of coral
flanked their sides, and they came to an immense
amphitheater of old Roman design. There were paths
paved with pearls and shells, forming a rich mosaic. A garden
of marine fruits and flowers moved delicately in the subtle current. All
about the fallen marbled columns were mer-folk, with little sea horses
dancing round their flaming, greenish hair.

It was then that Jack opened his mouth—in wonder. His surprise caused him to lose touch with Oolaloo. Water flooded his mouth. He was gasping and gagging. He looked up. The dome of light was too far off, too high to reach. He felt the cat's paws push him up toward the surface.

Too late, he thought, *we're drowning.*

Everything turned to swirls of violet.

"Come, come, lad," said a gingery voice in the bright air.

Jack stared into the gray-blue eyes of a fellow mariner.

"Will he live?" asked the captain of the ship, standing above.

"He'll keep," said the mariner, who was nearer.

Jack sat up. In his arms was a soaking wet tabby cat.

"You saved our ship's cat, all right," the captain said. "A brave deed, indeed. She jumped off the deck after a flying fish, and you went in and got her, lad."

"Luckily we heard you calling for help," chuckled the first mate.

Kit Cat purred.

"I knew it." Jack coughed. "Cats can't talk. Mer-girls ain't real." He looked foggily at the forecastle. "Was it all a dream, then? A spell?"

The captain and the first mate guffawed. "The salt didn't get his tongue, but it sure pickled his brain," the first mate quipped.

Jack shook his head. "Maybe it was real, at that. Oolaloo, and everything." He glanced at Kit Cat, who looked him steadily in the eye.

"That's the word you muttered when we drug you back on deck with this 'ere gaff hook," said the square-jawed first mate.

Jack grunted. "I never want to see another gaff hook as long as I live—especially no harpoon!"

"Oolaloo—what's that, Jack?" the captain said, ignoring the gaff remark.

However, Jack never told anyone what it meant. And though he became famous later on as a fierce pirate, he was kind to the sea people and all four-legged land dwellers. Moreover, he always kept a calico cat close at hand. And the cat's name had to be Kit Cat of Cat Key. If you don't believe this is true, look it up. Or better yet, ask your cat. They talk, you know.

Afterword

The ship's Shorthaired cat was usually a tortoiseshell. At one time she was considered such a powerful force against disaster that nineteenth-century maritime insurance companies wouldn't insure a cargo without the requisite cat-in-residence. This was still true as late as the mid-twentieth century in parts of the Pacific Rim.

For some reason, the tortoiseshell has always had some mysterious link to good fortune. Perhaps this came from the belief that cats, in general, control the weather. This was an ancient Egyptian belief, later carried forward to Europe. Indeed, when coastal weather was bad, superstitious sailors would place a tortoiseshell cat in an iron pot and put the lid on it until the thunder stopped.

The ship's cat that saves the day is a myth of long standing, proven by the many words that reflect this in our language. For example, there is the catboat, or, simply, the cat. The catamaran that rights itself in a turbulent sea is well founded on the feline faculty of always "landing on her feet." In Italian, the term gatta marina *refers to the boat that comes upright in rough surf. There is also the tackle, or pulleys, used to suspend the anchor to the— here we go again—cat's head of a ship.*

Moreover, there is the obvious myth of the sea-cat, or octopus. It was also thought to be nine-lived, like the cat after which it was named. Ursula, the sea-cat and witch woman in the Disney Studio animated feature The Little Mermaid, *is a perfect example of the legend. Norse myths of sea-cats are common. In Haitian voodoo, the sea-mother, Erzulie, has a watchcat for a friend, which goes back to African mythology.*

It's interesting, too, that the word "tortoiseshell" comes from tortoise, a creature of great longevity—not unlike the cat who is believed to have extra lives and who is thought to transcend the grave. The tortoiseshell is not a breed but, like the tabby, is a color pattern. Basically the breed may be an American or British Shorthair, but the coloration should be black and orange, plus one other color; therefore, a tricolored cat. Calico cats, like Jack's, are just tortoiseshells with white as the third color. This pattern is found almost exclusively in female cats.

Incidentally, the young pirate of our tale was the infamous Calico Jack, or Jack Rackham, a contemporary of the even more infamous Blackbeard. Both terrorized the Caribbean during the early years of the eighteenth century.

The Laughter of Cats: A Polynesian Legend

Long ago in the islands of the Pacific, where the sea turns violet at noon and where the palm-tufted mountains are rose-gold at dusk, there was born a *taupou*, or princess, the daughter of a great king and queen.

The princess was named Kaiulani, and soon after she was born, royal attendants placed her on a palm-fronded ark covered with hibiscus blossoms. She was carried aloft for all to see.

The people, full of good feeling, pressed round. Eagerly they thrust garlands of flowers at the ark as it passed. The earth was spattered with petals. On all sides, musicians, drummers, and flute players made wonderful sounds.

Now, at the front of the ark, Kaiulani's Siamese cat, Copra, was poised on a palanquin, or stand, of his own. Here was no ordinary, fish-stealing feline, but a cat whose lineage was as renowned as the princess's herself. The sovereign Siamese stood nobly, head high. He bore striking contrast to the bower of milk-white flowers upon which he was carried: brown mask face, sable paws, and rich, dark tail.

After many hours of feasting and drinking, Kaiulani was finally sheltered in a coral house on the island. There, with her cat, she would live in isolation for the rest of her life. Such was the plan of her parents, who couldn't bear to part with her beauty.

On the windward side of Kaiulani's palace was a wall of pink conch, very tall. On the lee side was a stake-sharpened bamboo fence that extended into the looking glass of the bay. Safe and secure, the little princess lived quietly with her devoted female servants. She wanted for nothing, and yet, when she'd grown into a lovely young woman, she realized she had no idea what lay beyond the walls of her impregnable prison. Every day, her parents visited her to regard the perfection of her face; but they never stayed for long.

All she knew was that she was a prisoner behind her own pleasant prison walls. In the dungeon below her bedroom, she heard at night the groans of some great monster that was her guardian. She tried to find out what it was, but all her attendants would tell her was that the thing was there to protect her. All night, while she was awake with her longing to be free, she could hear the clicking of the monster's teeth against the stone fortification of the dungeon. In the morning as the sea soughed, the clicking stopped and wasn't heard again until darkness fell.

Some days she caught glimpses of fishermen casting their nets at dawn and dusk, but she never saw them up close. Beside her, at all times, was her royal Siamese cat, Copra, so she was not really lonely for a companion. Yet she felt an emptiness, a yearning. She wanted to know, most of all, what was out there in the world at large. Was something waiting for her? The tapa-cloth mat that lay at her feet was decorated with legends, and she never tired of looking at it. Block printed and painted were tales of princes and princesses. Sometimes she imagined her own life, wild and free, in the dancing figures at her feet.

When she was permitted to go into the sunlight, she wore a woven palm-leaf basket over her head. This was so that no one—not even the birds flying overhead—could share her remarkable beauty. Thus did the king and queen shield Kaiulani from everything. Frequently the queen said, "How tragic if some young man should steal our only daughter, as the ancient story tells. Only a suitor who can best the monster and take his tooth could be worthy to take our Kaiulani."

Patting his copious belly, the king replied, "No such thing shall happen because, as I've ordained, our daughter shall never see anyone but her royal attendants. What mortal, I ask you, could defeat the creature we've installed in that dungeon?"

Selfishly they hid Kaiulani from the eyes of any and all, knowing her virtue couldn't be taken from them. However, they couldn't stop their daughter from dreaming—and dream she did—of a certain young man whose smile was like the pearls of the dawn sun. Never did she see his face, but only his beautiful smile.

"One day he will come to me," she said wistfully as she paced the length of her sweet-scented *pua* garden. The creamy yellow blossoms filled the air with their fragrance, but it was of no matter to the princess.

Her cat, Copra, blinked his china-blue eyes. "Perhaps," he said mysteriously, "the one that you wish for is on his way." But the empty sea held no promise except the myriad sparks of the copper sun.

As it happened, on a nearby island there was an ambitionless young fisherman whose name was Talolo. He, too, had a Siamese cat who was also of a talkative nature.

One day Talolo's soot-faced friend, whose name was Cowrie, said to him, "The time has come for you to find a wife."

Talolo shook his glistening black hair. His almond eyes shone. "I own nothing," he said, "but the *pao pao* canoe, which I made myself, and the wrap-around lavalava skirt that I wear. These alone are mine. What woman would want a man so unlucky? The days go by, and I cannot even catch a fish, let alone a woman. Besides, so poor a man has no need of a wife."

Cowrie smiled, and her whiskers curled against the brown waffles of her cheeks. Her frosted tail, black at the top, went up straight. "I know where you can find a wife," she declared. "But you forgot something important that you own."

"I did?"

"Yes. A most important thing—me."

"Pssht," Talolo said, smiling. "I don't need a wife."

He sat on the beach, head in hands. For a while he watched the little shells swirl away in the lacy tide only to rush back swiftly onto the hard-packed black sand. He was content, not wanting anything.

Cowrie put her forepaws against Talolo's knee. Her spacious blue eyes stared into his.

"I don't need a wife," Talolo repeated, looking away crossly.

"Trust me, you do," said Cowrie. "Come with me across the sea and I will prove you wrong."

In the end the persistent cat won out, and Talolo and Cowrie went off on a mystical voyage.

All round them the ocean swells heaved and fell, carrying their canoe, hissing across the deepest blue. Cowrie, in the prow, had her head aimed in the direction they were to go. Her dark-tipped tail stayed straight out in the wind. "We're not far now," Cowrie said.

"From where?"

"Don't paddle," Cowrie told him, "don't even steer, the sea will do it for us."

A palm-fringed island came into view, and soon they found themselves floating on their own shadow, as they drifted close to shore. The turquoise water shivered. But at one end of the bay a fortress of conch shells barred their way. Beyond it, going into the sea, a sharp-staked bamboo fence cut them off.

"Whoever put that up wants no visitors here," Talolo said.

"When you see her, you will see why," Cowrie said.

"See who?"

"Your wife. Now we must rest until moonrise."

Talolo grunted, going along with his cat's curious game. After refreshing himself with some coconut water, he stretched out on the sand and went to sleep. After a while Cowrie awakened him with a brush of her black-tipped tail. Talolo sat up and yawned.

"It is time," Cowrie said. She padded across the beach under the palms. Talolo followed, and they came to the great shell wall that seemed to have been sculpted out of the sea itself. Somewhere, out of the depths, came a hard clicking noise, as of an iron spike, or a tooth, striking against a rock. Only the omniscient cat knew what it was.

Before them lay the pretty, but impregnable, prison built by the fearful king and queen when their daughter was born. Behind these deep-set walls the lonely princess had dwindled away her young life.

Copra was staring at the moon-laned sea, and he started to pace back and forth. "Something is happening. I can feel it," he said.

Beautiful Kaiulani stopped brushing her hair. "What?"

Copra's whiskery face opened into a smile. "Something comes."

Outside the fortress the moon swam across the reef like a white-winged ray. Talolo and Cowrie stood on a coral-head, waiting for the right moment to enter the calm lagoon. The moon beckoned, but they stayed, hovering and watching.

Cowrie said, "Do you hear the awful clicking?"

From deep under the sea it came, and came again.

Click, clicket. Click, clacket.

"What is it?" Talolo asked his all-knowing cat.

"It is the thing you must conquer in order to win your wife."

Talolo scratched his head and shrugged.

Cowrie went on, "Your quest is to overcome a monster, so that you can win the hand of the princess."

"I'm no monster slayer," he protested.

"Trust me, as I told you before."

"I trust you," Talolo admitted. "It's myself I worry about."

Then Cowrie entered the moonwater.

Accordingly, Talolo followed her lead.

Straight away, Cowrie dived under the sea; hastily, Talolo came after. She passed through an underwater forest of staghorn coral. Below her an octopus cringed, its arms curling into a crevice.

Overhead, the surface of the sea was moon-burned into a flat, opaque

mirror of quicksilver. Below, a covey of angelfish darted, first one way, then another. Holding their breath, Cowrie and Talolo flashed through the glittery sides of the school of fish and came out on the other side of their silver curtain.

In front of them, now, was a cave. Cowrie, four paws stroking, swam into the inky darkness. Talolo came next, kicking hard with his feet. The tunnel arched up into a dungeon where outside air freshened the dripping upper dome of the cavelike place. They surfaced.

"We're not safe yet," the cat told Talolo as they stepped out of the water. She shook herself and shivered.

"What's up there?" Talolo asked, pointing ahead into the gloom.

A great wooden door, set seamlessly into the coral wall, blocked their passage.

"The monster awaits you on the other side of that door," Cowrie explained. Again, louder and nearer, they heard the noise.

Clicket, clacket.

"Well, do I just open the door and get myself killed? Or what?" Talolo asked.

Cowrie faced him roundly, her eyes glowing. "I have brought you here, Talolo. The rest is up to you. Do you wish always to be a poor fisherman, alone and without a wife? Or would you like to hold the hand of a princess?"

"Is it really my choice?"

"It is yours."

"Then the time has come for me to . . . do something!"

"It is your destiny," said the cat.

For the first time, Talolo found himself wanting something. He wanted to get to the other side of the door. He wanted to face his destiny, his adversary. But, most of all, he wished to hold the hand of a princess, if only for a moment.

Talolo listened to the terrible clicking on the other side of the door.

If I should lose my life, he thought, *it won't be because I let it pass me by. I see now that to have something, you must want something.*

Suddenly, his jaw set, his eyes hardened. In that moment he was no longer an aimless youth but a man, a warrior.

"Remember," Cowrie said, "you must kill the monster and take its tooth. Otherwise all will be lost."

Then, Talolo threw his weight against the huge door, and the salt-rimed wood gave way, crumbling.

On the other side of the opening rose up a hideous creature—a giant centipede with a towering head and clicking fangs that dripped with poison. As Talolo faced it, the creature extended itself to its full height. Then, rearing back, it jabbed its head at Talolo, who ducked low enough to avoid the scimitar teeth.

Cowrie cried, "Remember what I told you, Talolo!"

The huge creature recoiled, and again it swung its oblong, plaited head at Talolo's face.

Feinting out of its way, he mocked, "Hello, I've come for one of your teeth. Either one will do."

The black head reared, clicked, and prepared to strike. A thousand feet swarmed underneath the lower length of its sinuously armored frame.

Talolo and Cowrie were now backed against the wall. In front of them the centipede was weaving menacingly, recoiling for a final stab of death.

"Just give me one little tooth," Talolo said, his back pressing against the conch dungeon.

His right hand reached behind and felt a loose shell. He pried it free and, thrusting the flared, razor edge, swung it—just as the centipede struck down.

Swisshhtt!

The monster centipede's head rolled free of its body. As the headless creature writhed in circles, its myriad feet clawed the air. It rolled and lashed, then lay quivering and oozing, melting into the porous floor.

In another moment, all that was left of the monster was one black crystal tooth.

"Pick it up," said Cowrie.

Talolo took up the gleaming tooth in his hand. It shone like a dark diamond.

"Now, quickly, go up and out of this place."

A stairwell, aglow with coconut lamps, spiraled upward.

Talolo and Cowrie climbed it. At the top there was a vast room, twinkling with torches.

There, surrounded by incandescent coral, was Princess Kaiulani and her cat, Copra. They sat beside each other on a tapa-cloth mat covered with painted legends, one of which showed a figure battling a monster and stealing its tooth.

Talolo drew his breath. Never had he seen anyone more beautiful than Kaiulani. Nor had Cowrie ever seen a handsomer cat than Copra.

Kaiulani got to her feet and greeted them.

Then, for the longest time, Talolo and Kaiulani stared at each other. What they saw and what they thought, no one will ever know. But there is no doubt that they fell in love that very moment.

As for Cowrie and Copra, they rubbed their faces dreamily, purringly. They, too, were in love.

"I have never seen you before, yet I've known you from my earliest hour," Kaiulani said to Talolo.

"I wish to hold your hand in mine," Talolo said, his eyes transfixed by her beauty.

Then, Kaiulani suddenly got worried. "What will we do about my mother and father?" she asked.

"Do they have this tooth?" Talolo held up the black crystal fang that he'd taken from the monster.

Kaiulani laughed, but she was still unsure. Then her eyes fell to the carpet she stood upon. Beyond the figure of the monster slayer she saw a man and a woman sailing away in a *pao pao*. "Look," she said in awe, "it is written. He who holds the tooth must make me his bride."

The two cats, noses touching, laughed.

And that laughter, the laughter of cats, was like the music of shells singing on the tide. It is, they say, the very sound that tickles the fancy of destiny, bringing good fortune to all who hear it.

Indeed, it worked for Talolo and Kaiulani, for they lived together for the rest of their lives on their own deserted island. And the king and queen visited them no more than once in a blue, blue moon.

AFTERWORD

The cats of Talolo and Kaiulani have usually been depicted as Siamese. Not surprisingly, the breed seems to have drifted into the Pacific Basin from its former home of Siam. Also not unusual is the cat's fame as a swimmer, hunter, tree climber, talker, gardener, and all-around companion of humans. The sooty face, spine, and legs have been called "the shadow of an ancient god's hands." According to legend, a god picked up the pale cat and stroked it. The blessing of the deity's fingertips left a mark upon the cat that is considered sacred.

Other myths reveal that the Siamese learned to speak by being the guardian of princes and princesses. Furthermore, the kink in this cat's tail was supposed to have come from a thought it was told to remember—thus knotted, the tail was a memory tickler. However, another legend says that the Siamese was told to hold the gold rings of a certain princess. She placed them on her cat's tail, but they soon fell off. So the princess knotted the Siamese's tail to keep the rings from sliding off.

The outstanding physical feature of the Siamese is its coat. The contrasting color, from pale beige to chocolate brown, is called colorpoint. The points are the dark areas: mask, ears, feet, tail, and, to a lighter degree, top of the shoulders and back. The fur is short, the eyes are blue, oblique, and almond-shaped. The head should be a perfect triangle. This glossy, lank, medium-sized cat is full of energy and imagination. They say she reads minds and directs her well-honed intelligence to whatever she thinks is best for herself—and, of course, for us.

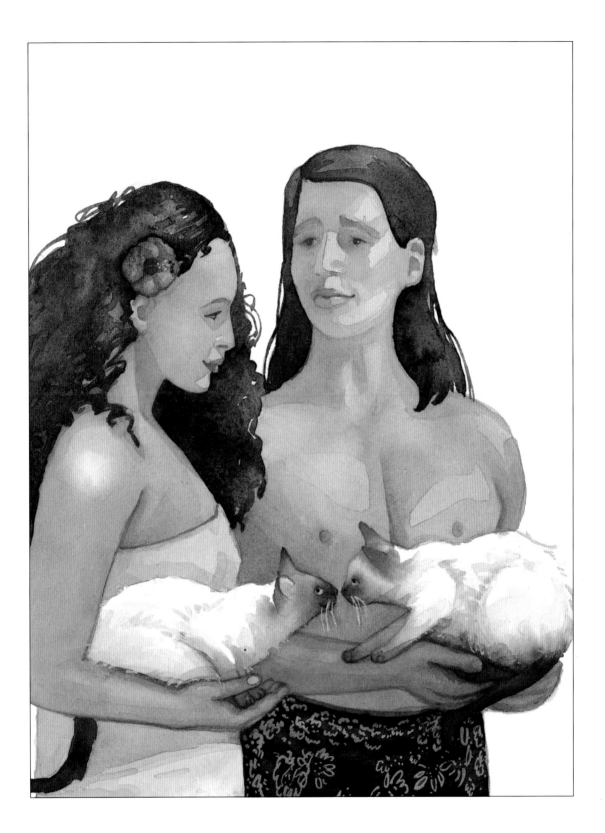

Notes and Sources

THE CREATION CAT

"The Tiger and the Tabby" is an adaptation from *Cats: A Celebration,* by Elizabeth Hamilton (Charles Scribner's Sons, 1979). This is a traditional East Indian folktale, which has been told in many different ways over the last century. An ancient and popular version once circulated in Persia and India. Our story is traceable to the Khasi Hills of Assam between Bengal and Burma.

THE TRICKSTER CAT

"The Troll King and the Butter Cat" is retold from a similar story in *The Mythology of Cats,* by Gerald and Loretta Hausman (St. Martin's Press, 1998). Praises are due to storyteller Roy Mackay of Castle Gordon, Jamaica, West Indies, for first telling us, "You can't tell the puss until you put out the butter," which started us on a search for this story. Carl Van Vechten mentions that this motif spans the entire Scandinavian world. Modern versions of the story occur in Warner Brothers' *Tom and Jerry* animated cartoons and also Warner Brothers' Looney Toons character of Sylvester the Cat.

"The Swordsman and the Cat" is retold from *Zen and Japanese Culture,* by Dr. Daisetz T. Suzuki (Princeton University Press, 1973). The manner in which this tale is told was inspired by our friend Janwillem van de Wettering, author of adult books about Zen and children's books about animals.

"Spiegel and the Cat's Grease" was inspired by *Die Leute von Seldwyla,* by Gottfried Keller (1856); also inspired by "Spiegel, das Katzchen" from *The Tiger in the House,* by Carl Van Vechten (Alfred A. Knopf, 1952).

THE GODDESS CAT

"Bast, the Cat Goddess" was retold from a historical anecdote in *The Life, History, and Magic of the Cat,* by Fernand Mery (Madison Square Press, 1969). The style of the narration was suggested by *Creatures of Light and Darkness,* by Roger Zelazny (Avon, 1970).

THE MONSTER CAT

"The Tale of the Whittle Cat" appears in many different texts: *The Cat in Legend and Myth, Volume 58,* by David Fitzgerald ("Belgravia," 1885); *Tunkashila: From the Birth of Turtle Island to the Blood of Wounded Knee,* by Gerald Hausman (St. Martin's Press, 1993); "The Gorging Cat" from *The Tiger in the House,* by Carl Van Vechten (Alfred A. Knopf, 1952); and from an unpublished translation of a Czech folktale, "The Whittle Boy," by Jan Wiener and Gerald Hausman (1973).

THE GUARDIAN CAT

"The Temple Cat of Lao-Tsun" is retold from *Cat Gossip, Volumes One and Two,* by H. C. Brooke (1928); also from *The Cat in Magic,* by M. Oldfield Howey (Bracken Books, 1993).

"Kit Kat of Cat Key" was adapted from *Wonderful Adventures on the Ocean: Being True Descriptions of Battles, Tempests, Shipwreck, and Perilous Encounters,* by Captain Hawser Martingale, a.k.a. J. S. Sleeper (Locke and Bubier, 1858). Jon Huntress gave us this book as a gift from his author-father's personal collection. Dr. Keith Huntress, Jon's father, made comments on a note card tucked into the flyleaf of the book: "J. S. Sleeper was known to have influenced Herman Melville."

"The Laughter of Cats" was inspired by Natalia Belting's story "The Fisherman's Cat" (Henry Holt, 1959). Helpful information also came from *The Life, History, and Magic of the Cat,* by Fernand Mery (Madison Square Press, 1969).

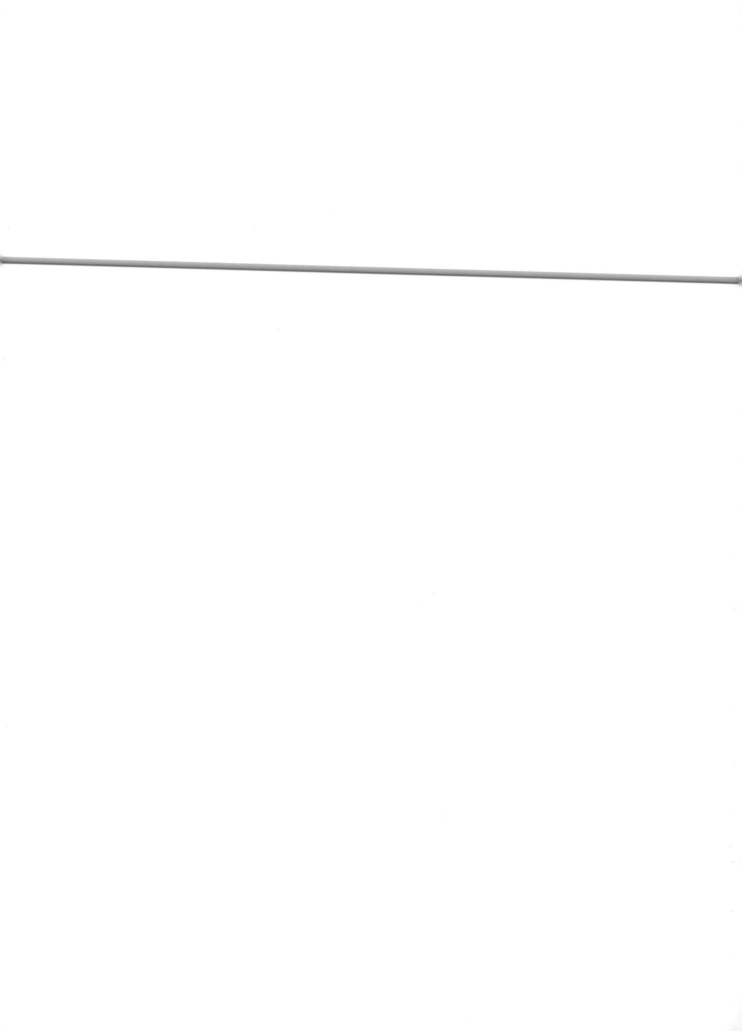